GONE ALASKA

Gone Alaska

A novel
by

DAVE BARRETT

Adelaide Books
New York / Lisbon
2019

GONE ALASKA

A novel

By Dave Barrett

Copyright © by Dave Barrett

Cover design © 2019 Adelaide Books

Published by Adelaide Books, New York / Lisbon

adelaidebooks.org

Editor-in-Chief

Stevan V. Nikolic

For any information, please address Adelaide Books

at info@adelaidebooks.org

or write to:

Adelaide Books

244 Fifth Ave. Suite D27

New York, NY, 10001

ISBN-10: 1950437787

ISBN-13: 978-1950437788

Printed in the United States of America

This book is dedicated to my sons, Conor and Samuel.

Contents

Chapter One

The Door Trick Game

In my hometown of Coeur d'Alene, Idaho, "going to Alaska" was an expression you heard often growing up. Alaska was where you could always go when things weren't working stateside. It was what the man or woman meant when they said, "The hell with it! The job . . . the wife . . . the husband . . . the kids . . . I'm cashing in my chips and going to Alaska!"

It seemed every family had someone who'd "gone Alaska" in their youth. In ours, it was my mother's brother, Uncle John. John was what the more righteous side of the family referred to as a no good drunken bum and, our more compassionate side, as a giant fun loving clown with a little drinking problem. Because children are generally better of heart than adults are, we only knew John as our favorite Uncle.

There was a Door-Trick game John played on us that I credit as planting the seed of some of these Alaska imaginings of my own—since I can remember him playing this game as far back as I can go. My younger brothers, sisters, cousins, and I would all be sleeping in the same room over at Uncle John and

Aunt Carol's house. The older people would be having a party in the living room and John would wander in around ten or eleven o'clock to say goodnight to us "pups," as he liked to call us.

"Hey, pups! Ya' haven't fallen asleep on me yet, have ya'?" John would whisper, loud enough to startle any of us that might be leaning in that direction.

"Uncle John! Uncle John!" a little chorus of our voices would whisper back from the dark.

John entered the room, all six foot seven of him silhouetted against a shaft of yellow light spilling in behind him from the hallway. Then, just as suddenly as he'd entered, the door would shut behind him.

"John? John? Are you there, John?" our little chorus would cry out.

No answer. Could it be that John had vanished? Perhaps he'd been sent to check if we were still awake and we had only imagined him entering our room?

But always, just before the hush of the room had driven us to complete hysteria, one of the little ones, for instance, would brave that ocean of dark hardwood floor and tug on John's knee, and whisper,

"John. I gotta go pee."

And the whole room would burst into laughter: John louder than all us kids combined.

After all the pillow tossings, ghost calls and who-pinched-who's had quieted, John would treat us to a long poem or story about the early trappers, prospectors and frontiersmen of the Yukon and Alaskan territories.

"Now just one mind you," John began, once a second hush had settled over the room.

My eyes would have adjusted to the dark by now. John would still be standing there—just inside the doorframe—perhaps cradling one of the smaller children in his hairy, bulky arms. His yesterday's clothes would be covered with sawdust and glue—the smell of the sawdust and glue and the whiskey on his breath permeating each dark molecule of air in the room. Years later, after John had once and for all been laid-off from Hoskin's Lumberyard, I remember this same John working as a clerk at my father's hardware store. I remember him standing behind the cash register, the bewilderment in his eyes—his big clumsy hands fumbling with the keys, dropping coins on the floor—and, finally at the end of that one and only horrendous week, socking the cash register, tearing off his apron and telling my father to take the damages out of his week's pay; John living off unemployment and Aunt Carol's nickel and dime tips at the HUSKY TRUCK STOP until his death of prostate cancer a year and a half later. Although some, such as my father, had looked on this as a failure on John's part, I had never seen it as such. To me, John had remained a hero: tarnished, but a man who's put his pride before pennies. Though I loved and respected my own father, when I was a child, I'd secretly wished I was one of John's kids.

> *"There are strange things done*
> *In the midnight sun*
> *By the men would moil for gold;*
> *The Artic trails have their secret tales*
> *That would make you blood run cold. . ."*

He would be speaking in that deep sing-song voice of his now. We would huddle closer: the smaller children shuffling across the hardwood floor in their sleeper pajamas with the padded feet . . . asking an older brother or sister to zip up their fronts . . . then conning them into sharing their sleeping bag. I, being one of the oldest, was often stuck with quieting a squirrelly younger sister or cousin: covering their small mouths with the palm of my hand; putting up with their wiggling, pinching, and drooling tricks so John could continue.

> *"The Northern Lights have known queer sights*
> *But the queerest they ever did see*
> *Was that night on the marge of Lake Lebarge*
> *I cremated Sam McGee. . ."*

"The Cremation of Sam McGee" by Robert Service was my favorite. Standing there, his huge frame reeling, his head up somewhere above the doorframe, John would "fill us in" on how he and Sam McGee were partners. Sam McGee was from Tennessee, and like John, had been lured to the Yukon and Alaska in search of gold. The only thing about Sam McGee was that he always complained about the cold. One particularly blizzardy night, Sam made John promise to cremate his last remains if he should die along the trail. Sure enough, next morning, ol' Sam was dead. Not wanting to break his promise, John lugged the frozen corpse of his friend across half the Yukon . . . until he came to the marge of Lake Lebarge. There, he happened upon an abandoned fishing boat:

> *"Some planks I tore from the cabin floor*
> *And I lit the boiler fire;*
> *Some coal I found that was lying around,*
> *And I heaped the fuel higher;*
> *The flames just soared, and the*
> *Furnace roared. . .*

> *. . . And I burrowed a hole*
> *In the glowing coal,*
> *And I stuffed in Sam McGee."*

John would purposively stop here, tuck the last of us into his or her sleeping bag and make for the door as if to exit. But always, just before he'd left the room, we'd demand to know what happened to Sam after John had stuffed him in the coals.

"WELL . . ." John continued, in his deepest bass yet. "I ain't quite sure I've figured that out myself yet." "Besides," he'd go on, checking over his shoulder as though someone was sneaking up on him, "I probably shouldn't tell you anymore–"

"Tell us, John! Tell us!"

"WELL. . ." the bass again. John would poke his head out the door; check up and down the hall, then, quietly closing the door behind him, tiptoe towards us with a finger to his lips, sshing us.

By this point, we were so riveted to John's story that I could often release the child I was holding. I can still see our eyes: wide and glittering in the dark: like a litter of wolf pups bunched together at the bottom of our den. Taking his regular stance, John explained he'd gone off for a walk, not wanting to hear the body of Sam McGee sizzling over the coals. Returning to the fire, he'd figured:

> *"I'll just take a peep inside.*
> *I guess he's cooked, and it's time I looked.*
> *Then the door I opened wide.*
>
> *And there sat Sam. Looking cool and calm*
> *in the heat of the furnace roar;*
> *And he wore a smile you could see a mile,*

and he said, "Please close that door.
It's fine in here, but I greatly fear
you'll let in the cold and storm—
Since I left Plumtree, down in Tennessee,
It's the first time I've been warm!"

Story over, we were free to let the cork off the bottle: screaming in unison at the top of our lungs. John fanned the flame by feigning to exit, opening and closing the bedroom door, then letting out his "grizzly bear roar" to let us know he was still with us. Our noise would overtake the noise from the party in the living room and, within moments, Aunt Carol or my mother would enter, reprimanding John for disturbing us kids with his "childish fool stories." And it was then, as I watched John exit, often playfully dragged out of the room on one of his big ears, that I knew I too would someday go north.

Chapter Two

Arrival

Elfin Cove, Alaska.

The Southeast Coast.

One month past my eighteenth birthday and I was standing at the forepeak, poised to leap, when the skipper of the purse seiner I'd hitched a ride on from Juneau motioned me back down.

"Adam!" the old fisherman yelled, leaving his position at the wheel and coming out on deck. "Your pack! You forgot your backpack!"

With the same haste I'd ascended the forepeak, I descended—grabbing my old external frame pack where I'd left it leaning against the wall of the wheelhouse. Grinning and shaking his head, Pete, the purse seiner's skipper, helped loop the back around my shoulders.

"Remember what I say. The Ivory Inn. Just as you get to the village. Can't miss it. Big white two story house with a white picket fence around it. You stop there first and get yourself a square meal . . . and a hot shower and shave in the rooms upstairs. Ain't no hurry, Adam. Nothing much going on till morning. This

Elfin fleet ain't going nowhere 'till King season opens two days from now. Turn down that idle of yours a notch or two, kid."

Pack on, I grabbed Pete's hand and shook it briskly.

"Got it, Pete. The Ivory Inn. First picket fence after you get off the Interstate. Big breakfast. Then shit, shower and shave—not necessarily in that order."

"Get out of here, kid!" Pete said, clobbering me over the head with his baseball cap.

I climbed back up on the forepeak.

"And don't ever forget," Pete said, shouting over the road of the diesel motor. "It's you that's doing them the favor?"

"Favor? What favor?"

Pete just smiled and shook his head. He pulled his deer-horn pipe out of a pocket of his windbreaker and lit up. A good old guy, this Pete! I remembered the trouble he'd expressed not being able to sign me on back in Juneau. But he already had a full crew waiting for him in Bristol Bay. It was only out of the goodness of his heart that he'd gone these ten miles off course to get me to this little village. Even now, I often wonder how differently things might have turned out had I got on with Pete and his Bristol Bay bunch.

"Never mind, Adam!" said Pete. "Big strapping kid like you—you'll do fine!"

Pete turned his short stocky frame around, and like a turtle standing on its hind legs, waddled his way back to the wheel.

"Elfin Cove!" I thought aloud.

The name could not have been perfect.

The village had been hidden from plain view, tucked deep inside this wandering bay at the northern tip of Chicagof Island on the west coast of Southeast Alaska. Now, as we swung around this last point, it came into full and sudden view. The entire village was strung along a single green-pained boardwalk that ran atop a narrow landing jutting up from the rocky shoreline, horseshoeing around the tiny cove like a railroad track upon the embankment of a river. Along the boardwalk stood a dozen odd shacks, a half-dozen supply stores, a laundry/shower shack, and one U.S. Post Office: like props from a child's train set. Moss, mushroom and lichen bloomed everywhere: upon the shorelines rocks and boulders; atop the boardwalk railing; even up the sides of many of the buildings. Ferns of varying size and shape and shade of green sprung from every corner. And surrounding it all, spring out of the soil of the village's very backyard, trees—mountains of them—Red and Yellow Cedars, Sitka Spruce and Douglas Fir; rising in a steep green cone; separating Elfin Cove and all that entered here from the rest of the world. Straight out of the Jules Verne and Robert Louis Stevenson books I'd read as a child. . .

"BROOOM! OOOM!"

Pete startled me with the horn, signaling me to jump. I could feel the seiner drop into low gear as I knelt beside the anchor windlass and regained my composure. Slowly, I stood up, and forced myself to smile back at Pete. My heart hammered in my chest and there was a strange wild taste of seawater in my mouth. The approaching land mass seemed at once to rush towards me and pull away. Grinning, I realized this was it. No running back to the Juneau construction job I'd worked for one month to get the necessary funds to make my way here. In my exuberance, I fancied this simple dock a kind of red carpet, rolled out at my feet.

Giving Pete a hardy thumbs up, I turned back around, and, staring straight in the face of destiny, jumped, realizing, of course, I shouldn't have the moment I had.

WHAM! I don't know if I blacked out or what, but the first thing I remember after the stars was the taste and actual feel of real salt water in my mouth and that half my face was underwater pasted against a board. Sputtering, I scrambled to my feet. The front of me was wringing wet. The dock had sunk underfoot the moment I touched down. Worse—it was sinking now—in front of me as well as behind! Goose bumps raced up the skin of my legs as I took several stone leaping strides for the ladder leading up to the boardwalk—icy fingers grabbing at my heels, spurring me on each step of the way. I didn't know what was worse: the dock swaying this way and that or my backpack swaying the same. It was like trying to run on a long balloon. The last plank snapped underfoot just as I grabbed hold of the first rung of the ladder. I climbed, praying that the rungs of this ancient ladder not break under my weight. Finally, gasping like a fish out of water, I landed myself on top of the boardwalk.

Loosening the cinches on my shoulder straps, I wrestled my way out of my overstuffed pack, booting it as I staggered to my feet.

"What the hell!" I yelled to Pete.

Looking down at the half-submerged dock, I wondered why Pete or I hadn't noticed the rotted-away quality of its boards. Hell—some of its boards were even missing! Back out to sea, I could just make out the bobbing figure of Pete waving goodbye. Probably pissing himself over how ridiculous I must have looked!

I waved back in spite of myself.

Grabbing a rock from beside the walkway, I winged it at a lone bald eagle perched atop a rusted gas drum across the way: the sole witness, outside of Pete and myself, of my botched-up stage entrance. The rock pinged off the drum's steel-casing, making the eagle jump.

I checked my mouth for loose teeth, my face for blood or splinters. Nothing. Everything intact. But there was a big bruise where my right cheekbone had kissed the wood.

I'd be taking a souvenir with me.

Chapter Three

The Ivory Inn

"The Lumberjack Special," I said, leaning forward and under my breath so the men seated around me couldn't hear. The Ivory Inn had no handout menus—just a single item breakfast written up on a chalkboard beside an old-fashioned milkshake blender: two eggs, two strips of bacon, hash browns, toast and coffee—for $8.00.

Ms. and Mr. Gloria and Harvey Boswell-Myers were the new proprietors of the Ivory Inn Hotel and Restaurant. They had me, and all the other customers, strung out along the counter like old-timers at the Veteran's Hall for Saturday Night Bingo. Ms. Proprietor was flying back and forth behind the counter calling out for refills of coffee while Mr. Proprietor ducked in and out of her armpit to whisk away their dishes the moment they'd gobbled down that last strip of bacon, running the dishes through the wash behind the grill, then charging back out to turn the potatoes, eggs and bacon on the skillet. All the customers, with the exception of me, were fishermen. Most were dressed in raingear and rubber boots. Their beards were unkempt; their faces pockmarked, the skin greasy on the surface but dry and weathered beneath. They sat hunched over their plates, shoveling their food, absently glancing at the television game show at a far end of the counter (coming through via the 12-foot satellite dish outside the Inn). Not many attempted to raise their voices above the brassy blare. They mumbled empty, fragmented statements to each other, leaving no doors open for response. I heard none of the boisterous, brawling vernacular I'd always associated with roughneck fishermen types.

The Inn itself was in process of renovation. Yards of plastic wrap hung along part of the ceiling and the far wall where I figured they'd stopped sheet rocking over the old plywood paneling. A separating wall, which I guessed had once divided the room, had been knocked out. Along the ceiling, a thick razor-like slash outlined the shape of the former section. In a far corner, shoved against the wall, was what I imagined to be a piano: a gray top covering it now. A small, twelve-by-twelve bandstand/dance floor was still standing, but they'd already begun to remove the mirrors fixed on the walls behind it.

My only guess was they hadn't gotten round to fixing the rooms upstairs yet. On my way back downstairs after a quick shave and change of clothes, I'd poked my head through a cracked door of one of the boarding rooms. The room was merely big enough for a double bed, a urinal and washbasin (at the same level as the urinal). The walls were made of cheap plywood so I imagine you'd hear the guy next door snoring as if he was in the room with you. There were no windows and no pictures hung from the walls. On the ceiling over the bed, a mirror covered a would-be boarder from head to foot. Strangest, and perhaps most revealing of all, the room came equipped with a small wall-sized jukebox: the sleazy neon glow from the box sending me hurrying back downstairs, wondering.

Ms. and Mr. Gloria and Harvey Boswell-Myers were an urban professional couple who'd come up to Elfin Cove in the spring from Washington, D.C. The State of Alaska had closed the previous management down last winter and couple had picked up the mortgage payments and would close the deal that coming fall. They'd come across the advertisement for the Inn in the back pages of the Atlantic Monthly magazine. Although still in a formative stage, a little hand-written note taped to the café window revealed the manifest intentions of the new management:

"THE IVORY INN'S JULY GRAND OPENING SPE-CIAL!!! TWO NIGHTS LODGING FOR THE PRICE OF ONE!!! MEALS INCLUDED IN PACKAGE!!! *PLUS* ONE FREE DEEP SEA FISHING EXCURSION ALLOWED EACH GUEST ABOARD THE IVORY INN'S OWN PRI-VATE VESSEL—THE SEA WOLF!!!"

The proprietors fed all this to us along with breakfast. I took it the fishermen had heard it before by the way they rushed through their meals and dismissed themselves from the Inn without further salutation.

"Are you just visiting Elfin Cove?" the proprietors asked me, after the others had cleared the room.

All the dirtied dishes had been cleared from the counter, stacked in the dishwasher, and were running through the wash. The counter had been wiped clean so not a crumb was left to prove that the fishermen had ever been there. The Breakfast Special had been erased and day's Lunch Special chalked up: a cheeseburger with fries for $9.50.

Mr. Proprietor had asked the questions and I instantly realized how much more I resembled Mr. Proprietor, with his frail white Yale graduate hands cleaning the coffee dispenser, than I did the fishermen staying at the Inn. Not one of them had said a word to me the entire time I'd been here.

"Well, in a way I am," I said, wondering if they'd noticed the shiner I'd taken pains to conceal by sitting at the far right end of the counter.

This was the summer before my freshmen year at the U of Idaho, in Moscow, and I was feeling that famous freshman itch to experience the "real world." When a high-school friend, Brian Connelly, asked if I'd want to spend the summer living out of his sister and brother-in-law's garage in Juneau, I had my bags packed and an Alaska map out before Connelly returned from his college placement exam. Anything to get out of another drab summer shuffling items up and down the dark dusty shelves of my father's hardware store back in Coeur d'Alene!

"Where from?" Mr. Proprietor asked, sitting down for the first time now to smoke on a stool behind the counter. The cigarette was one of those unfiltered ones from Amsterdam so popular with the liberal crowd at college coffeehouses. He smoked it now with his legs crossed European-style, careful not to exhale smoke in my direction.

"Excuse me?" I said.

The truth was I'd been staring at his wife. She sat in a little corner booth by the window now, reading a fashion magazine. The red and white picnic cloth curtains were drawn so every ounce of sunshine could squeeze in through the Windex-clear cafe windows. She looked up from her article as her husband repeated his question.

"Oh," I said, smiling sheepishly. "Idaho. Coeur d'Alene, Idaho. The northern part of the state—"

"Oh, I know where it is," he interrupted, smiling through his exhale. Then, to his wife, he added, "Hun," yes, he called her, hun! "Isn't that the little place with that magnificent hotel on that glorious lake?"

The Hotel Coeur d'Alene:

Once upon a time, there was a pretty little town on the north shore of one of the most beautiful lakes in the world. Each year thousands of tundra swans and hundreds of bald eagles came to roost on the lake's east end. There were black bear and mountain lion, elk and moose. There were salmon in the lake: trapped here decades ago when dams were built on the connecting Spokane and Columbia River waterways. Summers were the best time of year. The pungent smell of pine drifting through your open bedroom window on hot August nights. Cliff diving off Tubbs Hill into the lake in July. Lying down with your sweetheart on a bed of wild mountain strawberries on Mineral Ridge in June.

A wonderful place for a kid to grow up.

Then, a terrible secret was leaked, putting an end to all these childhood things.

Heavy-metals.

Lead.

Mercury.

Cadmium.

You name it.

The Silver Valley, east of my hometown and stretching all the way across the Idaho panhandle to the Montana border, had been one of the most heavily mined areas on the planet.

The EPA was telling us that 72 million tons of mining waste had entered rivers and creeks feeding directly into our beloved lake.

Those orange, yellow, and blue lake banks were not natural wonders, but the result of different metals and contaminants in the water.

Shock.

Denial.

Grief.

Enter Duane Hagedon and the great Hotel Coeur d' Alene makeover:

Hagedon, a Chicago real-estate developer, with enough money to buy a town.

And this is exactly what he did.

First, the pulp mill, our town's largest employer; then, the town newspaper. Suddenly, the key word here was no longer HEAVY METALS but IMAGE. Coeur d'Alene, Hagedon told us, would become the Lake Tahoe of the Pacific Northwest. He built this twenty-story, 450-room colossus next to the City Park and Beach: the Hotel Coeur d'Alene rising Deus Ex Machina on the beach-head like Poseidon to save (or destroy?) our town. The Hotel had all the makings of a medieval castle: a nine-hole golf course and "nature preserve" attached to its west end; a freshwater dock touted as the "largest west of the Mississippi" surrounding it like a moat; and, if this wasn't enough, an elaborate series of skywalks that reached out like tentacles from the Hotel to the downtown businesses.

He'd obtained highway funds from state legislators to widen all roads leading to Coeur d'Alene.

The Greyhound Dog Track on the Idaho/Washington border was fully operational.

Now all he needed to put Coeur d'Alene and his Tahoe of the Northwest into the 21st century was a few more legislators.

The lobby of his Hotel Coeur d'Alene eerily awaiting that day. . .electrical outlets already built into the walls at a distance of every two feet. "Well. . ." Mr. Proprietor continued, stubbing his cigarette in the tiny ashtray in his lap. "I'm impressed." Then, getting to the quick of it, asked,

"Then what brings you here to our humble cove?"

I swear, he said that.

Now his wife was staring at me. Her dark Italian eyes crawled over my thighs and hips, past my ribs, shoulders, neck, and, finally, face with a disturbingly measured gaze. I noticed she was smoking one of those unfiltered cigarettes herself now.

"Actually," I began, blushing stupidly in spite of myself. "I'm here to find work. On a boat. A fishing boat. A salmon trawler. . ."

There was an awkward stillness as husband and wife looked at each other and then back at me, unable to say a thing.

By near imperceptible degrees, I was aware that the sights of their eyes had lowered to the shiner on my right cheekbone, probably just now coming into what would soon become a full and purple bloom. I realized that they must have mistaken me of a potential long-term boarder: perhaps a rich college kid out here to study whales and climb glaciers and what-have-you!

Realizing I'd done something wrong, but for the life of me unable to think of a fitting response, I raised my empty cup off the tile counter.

The wife got up, motioning her husband to move aside. She lifted the coffee pot off the burner and refilled my cup.

I took a few complimentary sips. Then, slinging my backpack over my shoulder, I left the cafe through a side door; letting the screen door slam shut behind me.

Chapter Four

Philip Swanson

It was near noon and the crisp, sea-refrigerated air had evaporated from the Cove. The sun was hot, straight up, hovering above the inland ridge of mountains. I was on the rear deck of a trawler, down to my T-shirt. In my sweaty sunburnt hands was an electric drill, plugged into a portable generator on deck. Wiggling the drill bit back into its groove, I rammed it home through three inches of steel bar. I'd been cutting on this steel bar for the last hour.

The fishermen I found on the docks this morning were of a different spirit than the ones at the Ivory Inn. Like school children released onto a playground at recess, they jumped, hollered, cursed, and laughed while performing their tasks. The floating dock beside each trawler was piled high with odds and ends from their cabin's interiors: tin pots and pans, last year's dirty dishes, blood-stiff dishtowels, water warped rolls of toilet paper, coffee tins filled with rusted nuts and bolts and screws. Alongside these more domestic items, spread out in neat orderly rows, laid new spools of nylon fishing lines; rubber snubbers; different lengths of gaffs line out like sawed-off baseball bats; steel clothespins; black nylon stopper balls, flashers—and, of course, lures. Lures as shiny as new coins off the mint; detailed with day-glo florescent paints; with gaudy feathers and tassels and jewelry; even one custom jobber with a pornographic photo of a woman on it; anything and everything that might conceivably lure the eyes of those fabled sixty-pound Kings all were after.

Descending upon the docks fresh after breakfast, I felt as though I'd been spliced into a frame of old World War II newsreel footage. The fishermen moved in double-time around me. They'd paid me as much mind as they did the village dogs sniffing about (the dogs yelping and cowering as they were booted out of the path of a frenzied fisherman). All attention was drawn to the tasks at hand. There were poles to patch! ropes to splice! Even above, along the boardwalk, non-fishing village folk had been drawn outside the doors of their shops to behold the activity below. It soon became evident—after I'd been jolted a few times by a stiff shoulder or elbow—that the only way I was going to keep out of the icy harbor waters (that I was already so well acquainted with) was to join in with the seemingly frantic dance of these men as they bobbed and leaped from boat to dock and boat again.

More than once, as I'd tentatively approached skippers or trawlers to inquire about work, I'd been issue a command before I'd even a chance to blurt out my reason for being there:

"Just don't stand there with your thumb up your ass, boy! Toss me that line! Swing that dolly round here and help me with this crate! Quick! Turn off that faucet before we flood the forecastle! Goddang it, son! Move!"

And when I'd finally get around to announcing my reason for being there:

"Gosh damn, son. Damn it, I'm sorry. I figured. . ."

And down the line I'd go . . . running through the same routine on the next trawler.

Now that I'd finished the drill job, the skipper of this particular trawler I'd been working on magically resurfaced.

I could smell the whiskey on his jowly face as he reboarded. Motioning me aside, he wet the side of his thumb on his tongue and inspected the hole in the steel bar with it.

"Virgin, eh?" he said, smiling as he tasted the metal shavings.

"We do our best," I said, shrugging my shoulders.

Earlier, this skipper had hinted that there might be an opening aboard. As a matter of fact, he had restated, after taking a second look at me and praising me for my size and my youth—there was a damn good chance I could get on. Of course, first he'd have to check around town for his regular puller. In the meantime, there was this little drilling. . .

"Got some bad news," he continued, taking a nip off the strip of beef jerky he'd been gnawing on. "Looks like my man finally came in after all."

He offered me a nip of jerky.

I politely declined.

"Yep. Found the bum at Clancy's just now."

Clancy's! I thought, as I gathered my things on deck. My backpack felt as though its contents had been replaced with nuts and bolts. The drilling had corrugated the muscles of my upper back, shoulders and arms into what felt like one great anvil.

"Clancy's!" I thought again, this time aloud as I jumped down to the dock, my legs shaking beneath me.

Sure!

Why not?

This was the best lead I'd had all day.

And it was just in this state, as I trudged back towards the boardwalk and the village, that I, Adam Porter, caught sight of Philip Swanson and his salmon trawler, the Western World.

"Got a match?" was the first thing Swanson said to me.

I found Swanson sitting at the wheel of the Western World, almost Buddha-like with his feet propped up in semi-lotus position on the dashboard, fitting a joint he'd been smoking onto a roach clip. In spite of the 70 degree heat, he was wearing a copper-paint flecked sweatshirt overtop of a flannel shirt. Scattered across the wheelhouse floor were a dozen burnt matchsticks. He hadn't answered my first call from the docks, so I'd taken the liberty of climbing aboard.

"Light?" Swanson restated, politely enough.

From a side pocket of my backpack, I produced my Bic Lighter. I lowered the flame, and held it out as Swanson leaned forward to relight his joint.

Philip Swanson was not an easy man to look at. There was something unhuman to his appearance. His face had that granite quality which indicated he could be anywhere from thirty to fifty years of age. His skin was weathered as wood on an old boat; his eyes like two blue marbles that have been sanded so all that's left is a chalky pale blue core. His hands were stiff and white and always around his face: holding an earlobe or stroking his lips or his short beaky nose. His lips were thin and drawn tight at the mouth—as when two flaps of skin are held together with stitches on a cut. Because of this tightness of mouth, it was often hard to tell whether Philip Swanson was experiencing pain or pleasure whenever he smiled or laughed. But perhaps his most discriminating peculiarity was that one of Swanson's shoulders was set higher than the other. Later, I would learn that this was because of an accident from his early childhood. While aboard his father's trawler, they'd been caught in a sudden offshore storm during a run and, before his father had been able to draw in the lines, the gear had snagged onto a reef. Usually, when this happens, all it does is strip the expensive gear. But, in this case, it had snagged just so that it slipped one of the large trolling poles right out of its fitting. Young Philip had been cleaning the last of the catch on deck and had not been able dodge the falling timber in time. The wound had healed, and would not keep him from his work, but it had left him with a slight hitch in his walk. This too had added to the unhuman quality of the man. For, from a distance, one might easily imagine Swanson a puppet tied to strings from the riggings as moved about on deck.

"So," Swanson said, exhaling his smoke. "Where's the rifle?"

"Rifle?" I answered.

Grinning, shaking his head, Swanson leaned forward threateningly and said:

"The gun, dumb ass. The one my wife gave to you in Juneau. You remember my wife, don't you?"

I was completely taken aback.

"No," I said, shaking my head; realizing, by now, that he'd mistaken me for someone else. "You're wife never gave me your gun. I've never even met your wife. I think—"

But those two mentions of his "wife" must have done it for me. Next thing I knew my head was pinned up against a corner wall: facing a Pin-Up calendar of a topless dairy maid in the straw on all fours; playing the part of a cow, I suppose.

"Ss-stop it. Idiot—" I choked, trying to loosen Swanson's boney fingers from my neck. But it was no go. His hands were just too powerful for me. When I started to kick, he simply shoved his knee into my groin and held it there.

"I'm not him! Wrong guy!" I finally managed to say. "You got the wrong guy! Porter. My name's Adam Porter."

"Porter?" Swanson said, loosening his grip an nth of a degree. "You ain't from the agency?"

"No!"

Swanson let go of me so suddenly that I fell to the floor like a framed-picture slipping off a nail. Standing, nearly stumbling to the floor a second time over my famous backpack, I didn't know what was worse: the fact that I'd been attacked or that I'd been completely overpowered by this little man at least 30 pounds lighter than me but with a grip like a pit bull dog.

Apologizing, Swanson explained that he'd been waiting here three days for a puller he'd hired through an employment agency in Juneau. He'd had his wife give the guy his .30-06 rifle to bring with him. It was dumb ass stupid of himself, he told me, yet he'd gone ahead and done it anyway.

Rubbing my neck and collarbone, I tried my best to sympathize with him.

"Where you from?" Swanson asked, smiling as though our little scuffle was ancient history.

"Coeur d' Alene, Idaho," I said, looking round the room for a place I wouldn't need to stand hunched over.

"Coeur d' Alene!" Swanson said. "Ain't that up near that place where that Aryan Nations guy, Randy Weaver, got in that big shootout with those U.S. Tobacco and Firearms boys?"

"Yep," I said.

Swanson smiled big, obviously impressed.

A famous place, this hometown of mine.

Randy Weaver was a member of a growing organization in our neck of the woods known as the Aryan Nations; headed by a Reverend Butler, out of Hayden Lake, Idaho (about ten miles north of my hometown). The organization got its start, in part, because of an incident on the mountaintop property where Weaver lived with his wife and children and other Aryan Nation members. The ATF had attempted to get Weave to rat on the going-ons of his fellow members, and when he wouldn't, they decided to raid his mountaintop compound on illegal weapon sale charges. Of course, something went wrong. When the first wave of smoke had cleared, Weaver's 13-year old son and guard dog were dead and so was a deputy U.S. Marshal. 48-hours later, the standoff between Weaver and the ATF was national news. When ATF agents killed Weaver's wife with a sniper shot while she was holding her ten-month old daughter, even the most unsentimental of us found ourselves siding with Weaver. Why hadn't the ATF simply waited to arrest Weaver when he came to town? Why put the women and children at risk? There were even humorous moments: when the Weaver clan took a pot shot a news reporter Geraldo Rivera flying over top of the compound in a helicopter. The standoff had all the makings of the rugged individualist versus the Federal Government drama so popular especially here in the Wild Wild West. We watched ex-Green Beret, one time libertarian Presidential candidate Bo Gritz, walk like John Wayne into the Weaver camp and talk them into laying down their arms. Later, when Weaver finally surrendered, we watched this same Bo Gritz walking practically hand-in-hand with Reverend Butler and a small army of Weaver supporters coming down from the mountain at the end of the standoff. Suddenly, because of the media hoopla, our town was filled with skinheads from Seattle and Portland, Oregon and all points in between. It was a strange sight to see these tattooed, milky-white Nazis crawling over our beach turf like that maggots that they were; but it was horrible also, reminding us of the black Jewish student at the University of Idaho found swinging from a tree, his hands tied at the wrist behind him with bailing wire; or the explosion set off at the Catholic Church in Coeur d' Alene by the Aryan Nations two years before.

Great theatre, this.

"Hmm. . ." Swanson said, resuming his semi-lotus position on his stool. "Idaho. I like that. Last jackass I hired was from some preppy college back East—Dortmouth or Princetown or Harvard—something like that. Couldn't get a day's work out of him if I gave him a week. It was all 'what's this' and 'what's that' and 'what for' with him. All back talk and no back. Did us both a favor and fired him second day out. 'This is a fishing boat,' I told him, 'not a goddamn classroom.'"

It occurred to me that Swanson was getting round to offering me a job. Yet, in spite of the luck of such prospect, I was having second thoughts about signing on with this half-crazed dope smoking Weaver-sympathizer who'd practically crushed my voice box over a case of mistaken identity.

"Something wrong?" Swanson said, holding up his roach clip. "You don't go for this stuff?"

"No. I mean yes. I mean no I don't mind—"

"Good," Swanson interrupted. Then asked,

"Ever done any pulling before?"

"Pulling?" I repeated.

"Fishing?" Swanson restated.

"Sure," I said.

"What kind of fishing?"

"Oh, a little of everything, I guess. I mean I don't know how to fly fish or anything . . . but living by a lake like I do. . ."

Swanson or no Swanson, I knew I'd get stumped here when a skipper asked if I had any actual experience on a commercial boat. My actual experience of fishing in Couer d' Alene consisted largely of cutting the cobwebs that had gathered round my pole and gear each spring and then throwing it back in that same Godforsaken corner of the garage come mid-July: cursing my luck and vowing never to bother again.

I'd figured my actual lack of skills as a fisherman would be overlooked once they saw how big and dumb and ready I was to haul in them ropes or nets or whatever it was they used to catch the things with.

"How old are you?"

"Eighteen," I said. Then, thinking better of it, "I mean nineteen."

"Well," Swanson said, obviously having sport with me now. "Which one is it?"

"Eighteen," I said. "But I'll be nineteen—"

"O.K.," Swanson interrupted, grinning ear to ear. "Nineteen. Good enough." Then—leaning forward threateningly like when he'd asked me about his wife and the rifle—added:

"You ain't on the lam, are you?"

"Lam?" I repeated. "Like from the law?"

"Yeah," he said. "Any kind of criminal record?"

I shook my head, getting pissed with his third degree.

"How about a girl?"

"No," I said, continuing to shake my head.

"Big good-looking guy like you—"

"No."

Tapping his chin with one finger, Swanson said,

"'Cuz if you got some girl pregnant back home and go running off on me the minute you find out she's fucking Fat Joe—"

That did it. The hell with this! The hell with all these bloody fishermen! I'd take up some new hobby. . .maybe go out on that whale watch. . .get a job washing dishes at the Ivory Inn. . .see if I couldn't get back on the construction crew I'd quit in Juneau to come here in the first place.

And I was already one foot out the door when Philip Swanson called out:

"Hey, now! Hold your horses, kid! I was just trying to figure out what in the name of God's green earth gave you the notion of wandering out here to the edge of the world?"

I moved back inside the wheelhouse, my pack slumping on my shoulder.

"A job," I said. "What else?"

"Oh," Swanson said, letting his head fall a little on his chest so has face was at the same diagonal as mine. "Why didn't you say so in the beginning. . ."

He rolled up another joint. And we smoked it before he set me to salting herring out back.

Chapter Five

Red of 10,000 Years—
Cheesehead Pirates!

My late great Uncle John always said,

"There are three things you don't talk about in a bar. Religion. Politics. And SALMON. . ."

Even as far inland as North Idaho I'd been raised on salmon lore of the great runs before the dams. "Before the Dams" was a catch phrase from a time when Couer d' Alene lake banks and tributary stream bottoms burned day-glo red and green in the fall. "Before Grand Coulee came along. . ." Uncle John used to say. "The hearts and veins of these lakes and rivers burned RED with the blood and fury of spawning salmon. I'm told it was truly a sight to behold: like Monday Night football, 4th of July and an electric light show all rolled into one. . ."

I was ten years old when I witnessed one of these "light shows" for myself.

I'd been shipped out to spend the summer with some cousins that lived along the Clearwater River near Lewiston.

The Clearwater is a tributary of the Snake and, in those days, it still hosted one of the largest sockeyes runs east of the Cascade Range. For years I'd been hearing stories how my Uncle Albert harvested the fish with a pitchfork; how my cousins Bill and Ted "clobbered the critters" with boulders and baseball bats in the shallower pools; of the "infernal and unGodly stench of their spent and rotting carcasses" from Aunt Mabel.

All that August I'd awoke at the crack of dawn to walk down to the river's edge to see if the salmon had "moved in" during the night. (From Uncle Albert I'd learned that salmon move mostly at night. . .and I remember lying there in the coffin-like dark and quiet of the country night. . .thinking I could actually "feel" the salmon moving into their spawning redds the way you might "feel" an intruder entering your home.) All month this had been my morning ritual. And every morning . . . as I grumbled my way back from the river to the chicken yard to gather eggs for breakfast . . . I remember being disappointed by it. Aunt Mabel said she didn't know what was up. But every year the salmon were showing up later and later in the season. Uncle Albert said it was the dams and fish ladders on the Snake that was slowing them down. Bill and Ted—grinning and patting their baseball bats—said "the slimers" had gotten wind of what was coming their way.

Then, on Labor Day weekend, the morning before the day I was to return home, it happened. I remember it was a strangely overcast morning: clouds hanging so low I couldn't see the mountains in the distance. Thunder and lightning had rippled through the bedroom window all night long. I remember tiptoeing through the house . . . carrying my boots . . . and not putting them on until I was out of the back stoop past the kitchen door. (The last thing I wanted—should I be so lucky as to see these salmon– was Bill and Ted standing beside me, pelting the fish with rocks.) I had to climb down a mess of boulders to get a view of the river bottom. I remember the reflection of the red leaves from the sumac bushes along the opposite bank seeming more marked than usual. A dozen times I'd mistaken the shimmering of these sumac leaves for schools of sockeye. Then, reaching the big granite boulder that I'd singled out as my observation deck, I saw it. Beneath the RED of these Sumacs was another RED. A deeper RED. The RED Uncle John had spoken of. The RED of my dreams and streamside visions. RED of 10,000 years.

Up and down.

One side to the other.

Far as the eye could see.

SALMON.

"O.K. All right, already!" Swanson hollered out, lashing the last trolling pole into its fitting as I held the dangling pole aloft with block and tackle. "Now hold her! Steady . . . steady, damn it! . . . one second . . . one—there!"

Pole in place, Swanson bounded over to the dock to help me lower the block and tackle from the crosstrees.

We'd brought the new poles down for a fresh sanding and shellacking. Swanson had cut the forty-foot trolling poles out two Yellow Cedars in the front yard of his Juneau home: chopping down the trees in commemoration of the last mortgage payment he'd made on his trawler. He'd taken great pains to point out how the yellow wood of his poles stood out amidst the forest of graying poles around us.

"Just look at 'em!" Swanson exclaimed. "Ain't a slicker pair of poles out here this season. No, sir. Look around for yourself!"

Once again I grinned in acknowledgment. What else could I do today but grin? Less than 24 hours here on the coast and already a job on a salmon trawler! Brian Connelly had called me a "romantic fool" to give up digging foundations for his Uncle's construction company back in Juneau. He'd given me no more than a week before I arrived back in Juneau with my tail between my legs begging his Uncle for my job back.

"Mr. Brian Connelly," I could already hear myself saying after the long distance operator had hooked me up with Juneau. "Eat this!"

I was living the dream!

While we worked, I learned that the Western World was a 1940's Finn-built boat. Philip Swanson had known the original owner, builder and skipper, Hans Linderman, personally. Hans had been a vodka-drinking buddy of Philip Swanson's father. Swanson had even fished a summer aboard Linderman's trawler when still a boy (before the accident on his father's boat). Like Swanson's father, Hans Linderman had fished the coastal water of the North Pacific from Cape Foulweather, Oregon to Cape Fairweather, Alaska for almost 40 years (fishing more and more in Alaska as the salmon catch rates dwindled in Oregon and Washington states). Then, fall of 1986, the U.S. Coast Guard discovered the fifty-foot, twenty-ton trawler adrift off Cape Fairweather—unmanned. Noting the stove-in planks and the bruised, rotting carcass of the 180-pound halibut on the back deck. . .the official report on the 68 year old Linderman was he'd probably been caught unawares (vodka? senility?) and knocked overboard by the powerful tail of the halibut.

When I carelessly asked Swanson whether a fish could really toss a full-grown man overboard, he winked and answered,

"Guess you'll just have to wait and find out. . ."

Five years later Swanson happened upon the Western World dry-docked in Sitka, Alaska. A family of hippies had set up a commune aboard the trawler. The new flower-and-sandal bearing occupants had let Linderman's trawler "go to pot"— as Swanson put it. The trawler's bow and two trolling poles were missing; the galley stove-pipe was bent in the shape of an upside down L; the busted wheelhouse windows were sealed with yellowing newspaper and cardboard; and the anchor laid red and rusted in a clump of weeds sprouting up amidst the surrounding gravel. On the rear deck, naked children were playing on a tire swing hung from the steel hayrack—where the blocks and pulleys for the lines were formerly fastened. The new occupants had even given the trawler its name: spray-painting WESTERN WORLD across the paint-chipped in bright day-glo colors. (Hans Linderman, Swanson told me, had fished aboard the trawler for thirty years without bothering to give it an official title.)

Seeing Linderman's trawler in such disrepair, Swanson said he felt obligated to inquire within about the FOR SALE sign crudely spray-painted along the outer wall of the wheelhouse in the same day-glo colors. Six hours later, after a half-dozen of the first and best joints he'd ever smoked, the Western World was signed over in his name: three budding marijuana plants included. Ten years had passed, and Swanson had made his final mortgage payment this April. Now, he pointed out to me, all he had to do was pay off the string of loans he'd taken out for restoration and repairs.

"That it?" I said, dropping the heavy block and tackle in a wooden crate.

"That's it!" said Swanson, tossing me a rag to knock the sawdust off my hands and clothes. "We'll make a fisherman out of you yet!"

I accompanied Swanson up the narrow gangplank to the boardwalk and the Elfin General Store for supplies. Although it was eight o'clock in the evening, the sun was in the same position it had been at noon. Many trawlers were already shoving off for tomorrow's fishing grounds. Below me, deck hands loosed their trawlers from their moorings and leapt back aboard as their vessels inched away from the docks. Last minute bartering for needed but forgotten supplies were made between these soon to be competing fishermen: a roll of toilet paper here for a box of matches there. Some of the younger skippers had boom-blaster speakers hooked up to their stereos and they cranked the rock and rap music to spite the older fishermen:

"Ha! You play 'dat lout musik and scare my fish—I wreck you and yore boat out 'dare!"

And the youth's reply:

"Take it easy, ol' Sweedy! The soakers love it! Sets 'em off in a feeding frenzy!"

My shiner, which I'd taken such pains to conceal that morning, I now realized, was a badge of honor amongst these men. I was no longer ignored by them, but saluted as such myself:

"Better watch your step out there, Swanson. Big brawler you got there! Liable to chop you up and use you as bait!"

Everything was rolling my way! The antipathy I'd felt toward Philip Swanson had dissipated in the glow of the coming hunt: to such a degree, in fact, I was pleased to have him as my skipper. He was the perfect Wolf Larsen to my Humphrey Van Weydon! Ahab to my Ishmael! Names of shops, structures of buildings, positions of objects, patterns of traffic—which had set me off in such a panic when I'd first arrived—seemed suddenly familiar and most significant now. Clancy's Bar and Grill. . .that little patch of ferns growing atop the caved-in, rotted-out roof of the old outhouse behind Carol's Laundry and Shower Shack. . .that pile of rusted rebar lying tangled and half-submerged in the purple-tinted rocks and water below the boardwalk. . .the choking spluttering blast of an ancient diesel engine's carburetor firing up. . .two grizzly-bearded men bumping into each other outside the Elfin General Store—the one walking in, the other walking out—at first exchanging sneers and curses, then, upon recognizing each other in their new beards, exchanging hugs and tugs at each other's beards and HOW-THE-HELL-ARE-YA'S! All these things—all these sights, sounds, smells, voices, faces, gestures—mine because I'd joined up with Philip Swanson.

The Elfin General Store was as crowded with fishermen as it was with goods. We had to excuse ourselves just to get through the front door. A long line was formed at a right angle in front of the lone checkout stand: a broad shouldered woman with a red bandana across her forehead working the register. Fishermen and fisherwomen were dressed in flannel shirts torn at the elbow and greased at the sleeve; in baseball caps speckled with paint; sleeveless sweatshirts; overalls with one shoulder strap unbuckled; jeans hanging halfway down their crack. Those who weren't actually shopping or waiting in line were huddled around the magazine racks in collective disregard of the NO LOITERING signs overhead . . .sharing smiles and chuckles as they passed around porno magazines. . .the fisherwomen in on the jokes.

The walls of the store were painted olive green. All kinds of lists, charts and graphs were stapled there: Debt Lists for goods bought on credit (to be paid by season's end); Tide Table charts; Salinity charts; Geodetic survey charts advertising the best routes for trawlers to locate schools of salmon; a graph from the Environmental Protection Agency indicating the decline in catches over the years (this graph, I noticed, somewhat buried beneath the others). From the ceiling, a half-dozen bug zappers were hung like chandeliers. Because the one-room store had not storage area in back, the aisles were overstocked. Item was stacked atop item. If you wanted to get a can of cat food for your boat's cat, you'd first have to lift off the 10 lbs. bags of flour stacked atop it.

My father would have a heart attack if he saw this kind of clutter!

As we moved down the aisles, Swanson used me as a human shopping-cart. I was rapidly being buried beneath cans of peaches and pears, green beans and corn, soups and cereals; boxes of powdered milk; tins of coffee; cartons of eggs, dishwashing liquid; plastic wrap and aluminum foil. Swanson seemed to select the items randomly from the aisles—and stacked them upon me with the same indifference. The only way I even know which way to go was to follow the orang-utan-gait of the man in front of me who could only be Swanson. As a joke, I suggested:

"How about this bag of Oreo Cookies. . ."

Swanson, of course, acknowledged this as a "good idea"— adding them to the heap.

It occurred to me to protest in more obvious fashion, but, by this point, I feared a simple spoken word might send my food pyramid toppling to the floor.

"There," Swanson said finally, adding a handful of beef jerky and a sock of chewing tobacco from a display case in front of the checkout stand. "We're ready to go fishing, kid!"

And before I could maneuver my head past a box of Cheerios, Swanson shoved a wad of money in my shirt pocket and joined rank with his fellow fisher people at the magazine rack.

While I waited, I listened to a disagreement between three fishermen behind me:

"Fucking cheesehead pirates!" said the one with tobacco in his mouth. "They put a toll on me when I head down passage to Seattle in September and I'll put a bullet under the chin-strap of the first Mountie steps foot on my deck! $500 dollars—"

"Yeah—sure it's piracy! But that Tobin guy has a point. The Canucks kept their dams off the Fraser while we hooked up the Columbia like a frigging Christmas tree! A piece I read in the Seattle Times said we're taking a $100 million worth of their salmon for each 35 mill they take of ours—"

"Listen to Pat here!" said the third fisherman. "You're a regular Boy Scout, Patty, my boy! Discussing what's fair among thieves!"

"Thieves!" said Pat. "If that be the case—then even thieves have got to be fair—at least amongst each other!"

"Screw that!" answered the first speaker—spitting tobacco juice somewhere on the floor behind me. "It's dog-eat-dog, gents! Way of the world! If the Canucks don't like it . . . I say it's time we made 'em our 51st state!"

There was laughter and agreement over this last comment.

Chapter Six

First Morning

Now a day had gone by and I was sitting, half asleep, at the wheel of the Western World. It was four o' clock, opening morning of King salmon season, and I was supposed to steering us through some underwater reef I was supposed to see by watching this red light beep on and off around the depth gauge clock. Before I even had a chance to ask myself if any of this was really happening, Swanson came bouncing in the wheelhouse from out back and pried one of my hands loose from the wheel and placed three orangey pills in the palm of my hand.

"What are they?" I protested.

"Swallow 'em!"

He handed me a styro-foam cup with cold coffee in it. There was dirt sticking to the rim of the cup.

"Take it!"

I swigged the three little pills down. One stuck to the back of my throat. . .

"Good," Swanson said, flashing a yellow-toothed smile just as quick as he disappeared out back again.

Like a kid straddling a horse on his first merry-go-round, I scissored my legs around the legs of my stool. The sea heaved and sighed beneath us like one great lung. The wind howled out back. A chill crawled up the back of my neck from a draft leaking through the sliding wheelhouse door. It was still dark out: a blue dark like I was sitting in the cockpit of an airplane . . . taxiing around the runway awaiting a message from the control tower. The drag was in motion. The twenty-odd trawlers composing it, including us, were strung out about 70 yards apart; circling the inlet in oblong fashion as we hugged the opposing bank as long as possible before cutting across to the other side. Even though I sat here, going through the motions at the wheel, I had an uneasy sense that something was wrong.

Swanson came back inside—just in time to take the wheel from me before I ran into the trolling lines of the trawler in front of us.

"Jesus H. Christ, kid! Didn't you see that guy in front?"

"Of course!" I said. "I was following him just like you said I was supposed—"

"Scoot," Swanson said, meaning I had to lean my stool against the wall in this cramped corner of the wheelhouse. As Swanson worked the throttle up and down, his crippled shoulder kept jabbing close to my face. A thin trickle of tobacco juice was dribbling down the side of chin and the stench from his armpits was almost unbearable.

"Damn it!" Swanson cursed, jamming the throttle back into gear. I jerked my head back from his jabbing shoulder, smacking the back of my skull against the wall.

"Hey!" I said, rubbing the sore spot with one of my hands. "If you need me to move or something—"

Swanson signaled me to shut up, then flipped through several channels on the CB radio overhead and issued a few unanswered calls.

"Fucking williwaw. . ." Swanson mumbled to himself.

"Williwaw!" I repeated. "What's a fucking williwaw?"

Ignoring my lame attempt at a joke, Swanson dropped into the hull of the Western World, using the 5-step ladder leading down from the hatch.

It was the second time this morning Swanson had to re-adjust our course.

I swilled down the rest of the contents of my styro-foam cup, dirt and all.

I don't know what had gotten into me this morning. My coordination was all off; it was as though I'd woken up and suddenly discovered I was left-handed. Just seeing the other trawlers following each other in such neat 70-yard lengths should have been enough to tell me where to be and what to do. If I was too far behind, I needed to speed up . . . too close slow down.

Simple stuff.

Something a third-grader ought to be able to do.

A minute later, we were gain on the trawler in front again.

"Swanson" I whispered aloud.

I watched as the fisherman on the trawler in front of us came out of wheelhouse, waving his arms in distress. I thought of throwing the throttle into neutral, and then remembered that the trawler behind us was only fifty yards away.

Now the fisherman in the trawler in front was frantic: hopping around the rear of his trawler like a bee trapped in a jar. The fisherman's arm flapping intensified. I threw my arms up in a gesture of helplessness. He pointed towards center of the inlet.

"O.K.!" I shouted back, though only I could hear.

I steered towards the center of the inlet. Now I began to worry that the trawler behind us would take our position in the drag. With the drag linked as tight as it was, we'd wind up stuck in the middle of the inlet, absently swirling around with no way of getting back in the loop.

A rodeo clown surrounded by a herd of angry bulls.

"Swanson!" I called out at the top of my lungs.

Charging out back, I tried the same method of distress signaling the fisherman in front had used on the fisherman at the wheel of the trawler behind us now. But the trawler kept right on coming, the pilot unresponsive to my petition. For all I knew, he wasn't a real person at all, but the silhouette of a paper mache replica propped there to fool me.

"Asshole!"

I returned to the wheelhouse. I could feel Swanson hammering in the engine room directly beneath my boots. After several unanswered calls, I realized that the blare of the diesel engine so close to his ear must have drowned out all my pleas for help.

When Swanson did resurface, I'd steered us out to that spot in the middle of the inlet. Swanson didn't notice at first, concerned primarily with wiping the black engine grease off his arms and hands. He mentioned something about the idle being off kilter again when he suddenly realized our position and bolted out back with a loud cry.

Immediately I realized I'd done something wrong.

"The lines! The lines!" Swanson cried as he came charging back inside. He slapped my hands from the wheel and straightened our course again.

"You ran the two trolling lines together! I told you you can't turn too sharp or you'll tangle the lines up!"

"No you didn't," I said. "All you ever said was to follow—"

"Common sense!" Swanson screamed, throwing his arms up as he ran out back to look at the damage done once more.

"Bastard. . ." I mockingly scolded myself with a line from a black-and-white movie I couldn't remember the title of. "Now look at what you've done? Are you satisfied? Satisfied?"

"Look," Swanson said, returning to the wheelhouse to jerk me from the wheel.

He brought me out back.

"But the wheel? What if—"

"Never mind!" Swanson interrupted, his plyer-like grip on my elbow. "It'll guide itself now. Pay attention."

All trace of my sarcastic mood was obliterated as we came out on deck. Protected by the cover of the wheelhouse, the sea had seemed distinctly separate from me: much the way a road seems separate from the driver of a car. But out here on deck the sea lurched, whipped, and bucked about like the live creature that it is. It slipped by in great continuous rolls; some of it washing across deck, temporarily obscuring the surface we stood upon. If it wasn't for the handle Swanson had on me, I might well have gone over.

"Stand more flat-footed!" Swanson yelled, his mouth inches from my ear so some of his tobacco juice splattered on my face. "Get off your goddamn heels, man!"

The wind in the middle of the inlet was terrific. It ripped at the exposed flesh of hands and face. A flap of loosely furled steadying sail flapped spastically at the same level as my head so I had to lean over to hear Swanson speak.

"Now hear me once!" Swanson began, still holding the back of the elbow and still splattering tobacco juice on the side of my face. "I ain't got time to be repeating things to you!"

I nodded my head like a small boy to police officer. I tried to shove my freezing hands into the front pockets of my jeans, but Swanson shook my arm so violently I could not.

"There's two sets of lines! One's supposed to run out to the left of the wake, the other's supposed to run out to the right of the wake. One to the left, one to the right. If the trawler's turned too sharp to the left or too sharp to the right the trolling lines will cross."

Swanson paused, gesturing to the larger-than-life example staring us straight in the face.

"Like that!"

"Yes, I see that now. . ." I replied.

"Good."

He followed me back to the wheelhouse and informed our fellow fishermen over the CB radio of the little trouble were experiencing:

"Hey, wha- -going on–? Saw you drifting ou–. Must got— greeny—on—helm?"

The voices coming over the wire crackled, hissed, and squelched in and out as though being monitored by a censor.

"Green as they come!" Swanson answered, then flipped channel clear over to the other end of the dial so all that came across the air waves was a cold gray static.

"Comprende'?" Swanson said, looking at me and through me at the same time. "Next time we're out of the drag for the day. No ifs, ands or buts. Comprende'?"

"Comprende'."

I was greatly relieved when Swanson shut off the CB radio.

"One thing," I said, before Swanson set himself to bringing in the lines, untangling them, and restringing each one. "If I follow in a direct path behind the other trawler, I'll tailgate—"

"Weave!" Swanson interrupted. "Weave, goddamn it. But for Christ's sake, kid—not too sharp!"

And before I could even say oh or ah

Swanson was out there. . .hopping around in the cockpit at the extreme rear of the Western World like a man balanced atop a swaying fence. . .manually working the lines. . .the only thing between him, the ocean, mountains and sky. . .being two-feet of wood-siding he braced his shins against each time the boat pitched.

"Weave," I whispered aloud, a trace of a smile forming on my face.

Morning was on its way.

Chapter Seven

$4 Dollars a Pound

At eleven o' clock on our third day out Swanson ordered me out back to work the lines.

"I ain't paying you to sit on that stool like some kid on a Disneyland ride! I'm paying you to be a puller."

By now the idle had been properly timed. Swanson had even gone to the trouble of stringing a three-cornered piece of plywood in our wake as a drag board:

"We want to keep her down to two knots. Ain't no other way of going about it with Kings. The big bastards stay way down low . . . scratching their bellies along the bottom."

We were thirty miles south of Elfin Cove, free-trolling down Lisianski Inlet, en route to Pelican, Alaska. We'd left the spitting rain and williwaw winds miles behind us. The sky was a salty, distant blue. The steep red-shaled cliffs, which had helped produce the violent gusts of wind that first morning, were replaced by long rolling hills of Sitka Spruce and Western Hemlock. Dogwood, alder and various berry bushes crowded down to shoreline, providing cover for hundreds of hidden streams emptying out at water's edge. Sea otters lounged in beds of kelp along the bank. The clatter of their rock utensils, chiseling away on the shells of abalone for the succulent meat inside, carried clear across one side of Lisianski Inlet to the other. Mist curled up off the water and hovered a few feet above it in places. The nearest trawler was about 300 yards in front, another a half-mile behind going down the other way.

Swanson had granted me the "privilege" of attending the wheel these first 48-hours so I could get acquainted with my side duties about the Western World. First order of the day was to light the oil-burner stove in the hull and start a pot of coffee. Because Swanson had forgotten to get a new damper for the stovepipe's flue, it would become next to impossible to light it on blustery mornings. Between shifts, it was my duty to cook breakfast and dinners. Because there were better things I could be doing than standing around a stove all day, Swanson instructed me to cook things like canned beans and ravioli in the cans the came in: eating their contents out of the same cans to avoid dishes. He showed me how slow cook salmon: stuffing its open belly with chopped onions, potatoes, radishes—whatever—then wrapping the fish in aluminum foil and cooking it at a low temperature (in case extra work above deck kept us away from out regular meal hours). What Swanson hadn't taught me—or neglected to emphasize—were precautions I should take while performing these or any other seemingly obvious procedures. The night before, in haste to return to a task I was simultaneously engaged in above deck, I'd forgotten to remove the lid off a can of Boston Baked Beans before setting it on the burner and. . .upon returning to the stove after correcting the difficulty above . . . had practically blown my head off while attempting to open the heated contents after the fact.

But with the exception of the can of Boston Baked Beans and the tangling of the lines on opening morning, my first 48-hours had passed with little incident. Swanson's remark about the Disneyland ride wasn't far from the truth. At times I felt as though I was on an enchanted carnival ride: porpoises, like shiny metal torpedoes, played games of crisscross across our moving bow-point; humpback whales breached a hundred yards to stern like babes from a mother's womb; great pods of herring broke the sea's surface in shimmering waves of silver. And if this natural spectacle wasn't enough, the Western World's wheelhouse came equipped with all the accessories: a quadraphonic stereo with graphic equalizer and headphones; an impressive collection of mostly "stuck in the 70's" CDs and cassette tapes ranging from, on one side muscle-rockers like Creedence Clearwater Revival, ZZ Top and Mountain's "Mississippi Queen" to, on the flip side, country western faves like George Jones, Tammy Wynette and a Hank William's Jr. version of "Ain't Misbehavin'." And on the dashboard, in a plastic bag Swanson referred to as the "glad bag," the pot. Mother Nature's Dramamine and a fisherman's best friend! A half-ounce of it! Wonderful green sticky stuff that stayed stuck to your fingertips when you plucked it from the bag.

As I sauntered out back, expecting a leisurely stretch before moving to my new task, Swanson was in process of pounding the brains of a sixty-pound King salmon into breakfast porridge with the back of his gaff. The sixty-pound King had knocked itself and its dozen smaller comrades out of the 20-gallon picnic cooler (we used as a temporary storage bin before glazing the catch in the ice holds below deck).

"You-stinking-son-of-a-bitch!" Swanson shrieked, gesticulating each word separately between blows.

The salmon was a good four feet long. The smaller gaff Swanson had brought the fish aboard with was lodged in the salmon's side just beneath the gills. It hurked and jerked and pogoed its dime bright body across the slippery deck in defiance of Swanson's assault. I looked on in disbelief as two of the King's comrades were kicked across deck by Swanson's boots and flip-flopped to freedom over the two-inch high stretch of sluice railing. I made a tentative step forward. . .in hopes of retrieving the rest of the catch from a similar fate. . .then jumped back inside when Swanson and the sixty-pounder came whirling my way like two cocks in a cockfight.

Swanson was a man possessed. His gaff was an obscene blur as it came down on the head of the salmon again and again and again. I noticed—in a kind of horror—that Swanson's lips were set in the same savage sneer as the salmon's; his beady eyes burned with the same wild indignation; his forehead gathered in a white knot. The hitch of Swanson's high shoulder gave his body the look of a jackhammer-gone wild.

Overwhelmed, I returned the wheel. I felt fairly certain Swanson hadn't seen me standing there all google-eyed in the doorway. I would pretend not to have noticed because of the clamor of the motor and the music. I cranked the volume on the stereo; then, thinking better of it, plugged in the headphones and covered my ears with them. My shaky fingers were placing a fresh pinch of the green in my pipe when Swanson came barreling in like the world's biggest-Asshole parent, shouting,

"Get your ass out there and get them fish in the cooler! Now, damn it!"

He slapped the pipe out of my hands and ripped the headphones from my ears, then dropped below to the hull without another word.

I raced out back to salvage what remained of the catch.

The deck was smeared with blood and scales. The half-dozen remaining salmon were flinching and flopping all around me, gasping. I fell to my knees beside the carcass of the sixty-pound King just in time to get a clumsy hold of another fair-sized King attempting to flop the sluice railing. I half-carried, half-juggled the still kicking salmon to the cooler and dropped it in. The plug piece for the orange and white cooler had been knocked overboard during the scuffle and the little water left in it quickly dribbled out when I righted it.

Swanson emerged from the wheelhouse with an answer to the plug problem: shoving a hacked-off piece of carrot into the drain hole.

"Never mind," Swanson said, referring to the difficulty I was having gathering the catch. "Never mind! I'll take care of the catch. Grab a bucket. Start filling the cooler."

I grabbed the only bucket on deck: the same one we used as a toilet. I had the bucket, but hesitated whether I should use it for the catch.

"Look," Swanson said, grabbing the bucket out of my hands. "From over the side! See!"

Swanson scooped a bucketful from over the side, then poured it back out on the running waves.

"Is that too fucking much to ask?"

"I'm sorry," I said. "I thought I was supposed to use a clean bucket?"

"Wash it out!" interrupted Swanson. "And don't suppose. Don't be sorry. Just do it right the first time, dumb ass!"

It took everything I had not to answer back.

After refilling the 20-gallon cooler and giving the deck a quick swamping, I joined Swanson in the cockpit of the Western World.

The cockpit, sometimes referred to as "the turret" because of all the "flak" a puller gets back here, was a four by three by two foot sunken box at the extreme rear of the trawler. It was here, in this four by three by two foot wooden box I would spend fourteen hours a day for the next seven days hauling in the catch.

"Speed's the key out here!" Swanson began. "We want those lines in the water as much of the time as possible. Simple percentages. Each line here is capable of snagging four fish in one out. . .which means. . .including the second line. . .as max of eight fish at once! You follow me?"

I nodded.

"Think of this in dollars, kid. Eight twenty-pound Kings at $4 a pound adds up to $640 on a single out! Think of this when your arms are so tired you couldn't raise 'em if Miss America was shaking her tits in front of your face! Let alone wheel in another 200 pound load of fish! Think of the dollars then and all the time and it'll be all right. Even when it begins to sound like bullshit and, in fact, you know damn right it's bullshit—think about it anyway. In and out, kid! In and out! As soon as you get that soaker on board, you want the gear back in the water. Simple percentages."

Swanson had me stand back now and watch. He explained how the two trolling poles were hooked up to blocks and pulleys hanging from the gurdie's steel hayrack. He showed me how to set and release the brake when reeling in and reeling out the trolling lines with the gurdy crank. He showed me how to unclip the four tag-lines from the main trolling line by their steel clothespins and how to be sure to thread the tag-line in with my fingertips only:

"None of this wrapping the line round your palm shit. A one-handed puller won't do me no good."

Swanson made a gesture of a hand sliced by the blade-thin nylon line.

After each tag-line was secured, I was instructed to neatly lay the coiled-up line along the fender of the trawler. Then, after I'd brought all four tag-lines in, I could quickly rebait the hooks (with the salted herrings in the bucket beside me), clip the tag-lines back onto the main trolling line, run it back out, and side-step it over to the other trolling line.

"Remember," Swanson said. "Speed's the key! In and out. And don't ever forget—when it gets tough out here—it's the dollars you're back here for. The dollars when it's tough!"

"Right," I said, already reaching over the water for my first tag-line.

"Oh, yeah" Swanson said, as though an afterthought. "Watch them swells. Don't have yourself leaning to far out on top of one. Let it pass first. When I'm sitting up there at the wheel I sometimes don't look back for a half-hour at a time. By that time I'm afraid—"

"Right," I said, grabbing onto the hayrack as one of those swells passed. "Guess that water's colder than it looks."

"She's a cold bitch, all right," Swanson replied, flashing a rare smile. "Now you're getting it!"

And for the next three hours I ran the trolling lines in and out at a furious clip. Swanson sat at the wheel with his ever-present pipe and Hustler magazine in his lap and gave me a thumb's up progress report from time to time.

Not once did he let me in on the fact that most of the salmon were bedded down for their noon siesta and that it was highly unlikely I'd snag even one. . .

At $4 dollars a pound. . .

Chapter Eight

Miss Sue Ann Bonnet

I was packing the catch in the ice holds below deck when Old Judge Peterson and his half-crazy, half-Tlingit Indian daughter-in-law, Miss Sue Ann Bonnet, sidled up to the Western World in their purple, plastic skiff. I'd poked my head above deck just in time to see Swanson greet our dinner guests: down on a knee with one hand bracing the shaky skiff alongside the trawler and the other extended to give our guests something to climb aboard with.

"Thank you, Philip," said Miss Sue Ann Bonnet, climbing aboard with the measured grace of a true lady boarding a yacht.

Old Judge Peterson's boarding was more difficult. He was a large man with a bum-leg that fell asleep on him when bent-up in one position for too long. Such was the case now as I watched Swanson and Miss Sue Ann Bonnet drag him out of the skiff.

"Keerist, almighty!" Old Judge Peterson bellowed, once they'd flopped his six-foot seven carcass onto the damp deck.

The old man staggered to his feet, spanking the flat of his dead leg's foot on the deck in goose-step fashion to get the circulation going again. "Keerist! Where's that big greenhorn I thought I saw working the lines for you the other day? Did he up and scare off on you already, Phil?"

At this mention of me, I quickly ducked back below to my chores.

We were anchored in a quiet little cove five miles north of Pelican, Alaska. With our engine shut down, poles stacked up, and lines drawn in, we, and the thirty-odd trawlers assembled here, resembled a congregation of rented rowboats on the first day of fishing season back home. Fragments of conversations from our lamp-lit wheelhouses skipped and scattered across the dark, still water of the cove. Bald eagles lined the tops of dark green Cedars along shore, waiting to see what surprises we slopped out on the waters from a day's worth of garbage tonight. Black, molecular-like clouds of mosquitoes drifted from trawler to trawler: seeking out boats that had neglected to spray the outer wall of its wheelhouse with insect repellant. The weather and the fishing had been so good we'd anchored in this cove for three nights running—putting off our stopover in Pelican for the time being.

"Naw," I heard Swanson say. "I ain't figured this one out yet. It's like he should have run off days ago . . . yet . . . somehow . . . he's still around. Been almost a week! Got him down packing the catch right now."

"Well, just goes to show," Old Judge Peterson said, still stamping his leg about. "A fella just can't tell with these kids nowadays. Flighty as a young gal with too many suitors! Don't got that stick-to-iveness my generation had—or yours, I suppose. Just never can tell. Ain't that so, Miss Sue Ann Bonnet? Sue Ann?"

Miss Sue Ann Bonnet was standing directly above me: but to that side of the hatch so I could only see her shadow cast by the deck lights overhead. From her shadow, I could see that she was absently twirling a long lock of her hair with a forefinger.

"Oh, Miss Sue Ann Bonnet?" I heard Old Judge Peterson say as his shadow put a gentle arm around Sue Ann's shoulders. "Won't you come join us for dinner? Let the boy finish his chores so he can join us when he's done."

And without protest, I watched Sue Ann's shadow move off with Old Judge Peterson's as their footsteps followed Swanson's down to the hull.

Hurriedly, I stuffed chopped ice into the slit bellies of the last half-dozen salmon, simply using what would lie in the open palms of my numb hands. Whereas I usually stacked the salmon neatly like cords of wood along the bulwark, I carelessly chucked these last half-dozen any which way atop the current pile, intending to straighten them later. This much done, I scurried up the ladder leading out of the shadowy holds, wondering what I'd already missed.

"I've a feeling you'll get a kick out of these two. . ." Swanson had informed me that afternoon during a lull out back.

"Old Judge Peterson's been here as long as any of these old Scandies. Didn't come up from the old country though. Came up from a little one-horse town of Jackfork, Oklahoma! Or—excuse me—the little one mule town of Jackass, Okie-homa—as Peterson puts it! Came up during the early 30's. . .was up in '36 when they set the all-time record salmon catch of 126 million fish! This was before technology, kid! Before depth gauges, CB radios, hydraulic power blocks! Hell, yes! I'd give me left nut to be in on something like that. No closure dates. No regulatory commissions. No Indians whining about treaty rights. None of these enviro-fascists from California telling us Alaskans what we can do with our fish! Just pure fishing, kid . . . pure fishing. . ."

". . . and wait'll you get hold of Miss Sue Ann Bonnet! Little crazy, but a real looker. That ain't her real name—Sue Ann Bonnet. That's the name Old Judge Peterson's son, George, gave her when they wed. Father was some kind of chief—Old Crazy Eyes—something. Mother a Swedish whore. Claims she's some kind of witch-shaman—something. Goes on and on about Mother Earth and Father Sky—about the end of the white man's world and new dawn of the Indian's—that sorta shit. Real looker though! And a good sport. Did a little dancing up in Dutch Harbor before her and George Peterson wed . . . if you know what I mean."

The halibut was rolled in a thick yellow dough that tasted like donut. The warm white meat inside had a strange, sweet flavor that was surprisingly not fishy. After five days of eating salmon smoked, baked, fried and reheated as leftovers, the halibut tasted like the most marvelous dish in the world. I scraped my paper plate clean as I watched Miss Sue Ann Bonnet pour fresh brewed coffee into three styro-foam cups.

Sue Ann handed a steaming cup to me. I was sitting on the floor next to the stove with my back braced against the baseboard of the Western World's sleeping birth.

"It's cowboy coffee!" Sue Ann said, apologizing for the coffee grinds swirling around the top and clinging to the inside of the cup. "You're supposed to use the grinds like tabacca. See!"

She tucked her tongue under the corner of her bottom lip so it looked like a plug of tobacco was underneath.

"Worked my first summer on a purse seiner out of Ketchikan!" Judge Peterson continued. "These here modern boats are luxury-liners compared to what we worked on in those days. We had to haul our own anchor, chop our own wood for the stove. Didn't have no hydraulic power blocks bringing the nets right up to the boat! Had to haul the catch every inch of the way! Our hands would be so balled-shut in the morning from gripping and pulling and twisting on them raw Manila nets we'd have to soak 'em in bowls of whiskey just to get 'em moving again. Then we'd chug-a-lug what was left in the bowls to make us dumb enough to go out and do it all over again! One of these fellas had a still hooked-up to his stove, see. . ."

Miss Sue Ann Bonnet was staring at me with a dark thoughtful expression on her face. When I smiled at her, she did not smile back. I looked away, trying me best to concentrate on Old Judge Peterson's words, the whiskey already taking effect.

"Yes, siree, Adam, my boy! We were an all-around different breed of man back then. Tougher, maybe. Not so much 'cuz we was born tougher . . . as we became tougher by just surviving the world we was living in then. Do you follow me, Adam?"

I nodded, refilling my own cup this time.

"We was coming out of the Depression then. . ."

When I motioned Sue Ann with the bottle for more whiskey, she again showed no sign of recognition . . . just this far-away staring.

". . . those of us who came up—and lasted—weren't necessarily looking to get rich. A little food in our bellies . . . some clothes on our backs . . . and we was happy as a lark! If there was anything left over . . . well . . . that was allotted to what you might refer to as the 'candy fund'."

He squeezed Sue Ann Bonnet's leg good-naturedly.

"Those of us who stuck around generally broke ties with our kin. We were sorta cut off up here, see. No phones. No jet planes. As for mail service then. . ." He grunted and made a waving gesture with one of his big arms. "Might as well stick your letter in a bottle! If any of the fellas received a 'Dear John' letter . . . chances were he wouldn't find out about it till he'd plum forgotten what that little farm gal that had him in such a whirl looked like in the first place!"

At this time, Swanson's crooked figure came clambering back down the 5-step ladder. He had that strange half-smile, half-grimace on his face. There was a Philip's screwdriver in his hand.

"Sorry to cut in on the soap box, old man," Swanson said. "But I need an extra pair of hands on a busted exhaust hose . . . and since my new puller here's off-duty—"

"At your service, Captain!" Peterson bellowed, leaping off his upended bucket so fast I was amazed he hadn't cracked his head on the low ceiling.

"That's all right, Judge," I said. "I'll help with the hose. You and Sue Ann just relax while I—"

"No," Judge Peterson said, holding me back with one of his giant hands. "Rest up, Adam. It's good for an old dog to be of service!"

While Swanson and Judge Peterson fussed over the exhaust hose at the other end of the hull, Sue Ann and I watched. Some of the sparkle had returned to her eye, but I was still curious to know what she had been thinking about during Peterson's monologue. When she accepted my second offer of more whiskey, I noticed that alongside the diamond wedding ring on her finger she wore a thin, gold band. It was one of those cheap promise rings I'd seen on a few girls back home at high school. I wondered why she still wore it. From my limited savvy on these matters, I'd always thought the woman took off the promise ring when she got the wedding band.

"Why don't you two go up for some air," Swanson suggested, "Better than sitting there like a couple of kids on a blind date!"

I helped Sue Ann clean up the paper plates, cups and utensils. Then I followed her above deck.

A big yellow moon was hanging over the cove as we came out on deck. Sue Ann made her way to rear of the trawler, standing beside the galvanized pipes of the steel hayrack. I sat on the lidded picnic cooler and lit the joint I'd been carrying in the back pocket of my jeans since that morning. The joint was damp and it took a few flicks from my lighter before I got it going O.K.

Sue Ann removed her bandana now, letting her raven-colored hair fall to the middle of her back. The midnight breeze coming off the open channel loosened and played with individual strands of her hair so they moved like thin, electric shadows across the side of her face. She did not push them back from her face. She was staring towards the wooded shore. I noticed that that same dark, melancholy look had returned to her eye and seeing this made me shiver. I took one more toke, then passed it on to Sue Ann Bonnet.

I became aware of the Western World slowly rotating on its anchor. Our deck lights had been turned off. Only a few trawlers anchored here still had any lights on. From a trawler in towards shore, I could hear the faint, electric twang of a country-western song. Outside of this, the only other sounds I heard were the plastic skiff bumping up against the rib of the Western World and Judge Peterson and Philip Swanson joking and cussing from the hull.

"Listen!" Miss Sue Ann Bonnet said, in a hushed whisper. "Along shore!"

Spooked from my reverie, I straightened on the cooler. Sue Ann had moved past the hayrack to the edge of the boat, one foot on the sluice railing and an arm around a steel cable.

"Listen to what?" I said, after a pause. I expected to hear a bear or deer breaking through the brush along shore; or maybe a pod of Orcas blowing somewhere out on the channel. But I heard none of these sounds. Just the same ones from before.

"Sssh!" Sue Ann answered, still leaning over the side of the boat. "The trees, Adam! You can hear them crying!"

Looking towards shore, I could just discern the subtle swaying of great trunks in the blue light.

"Yeah. . ." I said, holding in a long toke. "I hear the trees creak. Their creaking sounds nice."

"No, Adam!" Sue Ann said—the urgency in her voice making me cough a little as smoke escaped my lungs. "Listen with you heart, not your ears. Listen closer."

I stared down into the black green waters and, for a moment, the sound of the great trunks swaying did sound more like crying than creaking.

"Wow. . ." I heard myself saying in the same hushed whisper. "I hear it now. A second sound: like people murmuring and crying softly at a funeral."

I looked in towards the yellow light overflowing into the wheelhouse from the hull. Judge Peterson and Swanson's cursing and banging-away on things rose up from the engine room as before: and I was struck how they were part of a very different world than the one Miss Sue Ann Bonnet and me were experiencing here on deck—if only for a moment.

"Wild stuff," I said, passing the joint to Sue Ann again. "Kind of spooky. But if all living things have feeling . . . and a tree is a living thing . . . I suppose it has as much right to cry as the rest of us."

Now Sue Ann was crying and laughing at the same time. She took a long hit, so the end of the joint lit up cherry red.

"You all right?" I said. I made to get up . . . go to her . . . but remained seated when Sue Ann motioned me to remain so.

"Yes," she said, laughing again. She wiped her nose with the back of her hand. "It's this goddamn dope. That . . . and you remind me of someone I knew a long time ago."

I began to ask her who this was, but stopped when she shook her head to signify the subject was off-limits.

She sat beside me on the cooler.

"Thank you," Sue Ann said, taking hold of my hand. "I feel better now."

I could feel the warmth of her body next to mind and feeling this made me shiver. When she turned towards me, her eyes were still soft and wet from crying. She looked into my eyes and I into hers and—for an instant—I was sure we were going to kiss. Then, just when I thought she really would kiss me, she looked away—breaking out in a loud, but warm laugh that made me laugh unknowingly along with her.

"Oh, Adam. . ."

When her laughter died down to a few snorting chuckles, she threw an arm over my shoulder and kissed me on the cheek.

"You're a beautiful young man!" she said, mussing with my hair a little now. "Christ—if I was a young woman again—I wouldn't let you out of my sight for a minute!"

I smiled.

Then she said something that made me stop smiling:

"Adam, get out of this place!"

Just like that: point blank.

"What?"

"This place!" she repeated, throwing her hands up and looking round us. "I know how wonderful and beautiful all this is . . . but, truth is, we are killing the thing we all love by fishing it so hard it can't sustain itself. I've seen so many boats on Bristol Bay the night before a sockeye run that it's lit up like a floating city. We take every salmon we can get . . . and then wonder why each year the fish counts get lower. The Canucks blame it on the Americans, the Americans blame it on the Canucks—, and everyone blames it on the tribes. But we are all to blame! No one is willing to step back and give Mother Earth a chance to heal herself. We take and take and take. . ."

She paused to finish tying her bandana around her hair again, and then continued:

"When I was just a little older than you, Adam, they sent me to a 'rehabilitation center'. They made me read this novel by this funny Russian author whose name I can't remember or even pronounce—Dog Sty or Dog Wesky?"

"Dostoevsky?" I asked.

"That's it!" Miss Sue Ann said, her large brown eyes lighting up when she smiled. "I knew you were a smart kid, Adam! Though I still can't pronounce the damn name right!"

I smiled back, laughing a little at Sue Ann calling the great Russian writer Dog Wesky!

That was pretty funny!

"Anyhow!" Sue Ann continued, serious again—her eyes scolding me. "I remember this line from the book. It said the hardest thing for a person to do is take a new step—a truly new step! And that damn Ruskie is right! Because we are all such creatures of habit!"

She coughed lightly, covering her mouth with a fist. She paused, a look on her face like she had suddenly seen something she remembered—maybe a ghost from her past? – and then, just as suddenly, it was gone again. She shook her head and continued:

"But I did it, Adam. I changed my wild and wanton ways! It was the hardest thing I ever did—but I did it. And if I hadn't. . .I'd have never have met a truly great guy like my husband, George! Taking this step is hard as hell, Mr. Adam Porter. But it can be done. Take it from me—a gal who knows!

The breeze coming in from the open channel was stronger now, and crying from the trees along shore was louder than ever.

"Adam?" Sue Ann said, sitting up straight on the cooler. "Can you promise one thing?"

"Sure," I said.

"Promise you'll consider what I'm telling you tonight. I know it's not as simple as I'm making it—we all have bills to pay, roofs to keep, kids to feed—but there has to be a better way. We've got to put Mother Earth first, give her time to heal so they'll be something for future generations. Alaska is not a whore, Adam. It's not something to hump and dump on. We've got all the gold-diggers we need. If this is why you're here . . . then go back, Adam Porter. Go back to wherever it is you come from and see if you can't heal the place you're from! Take that step! Be that change! Promise —"

Suddenly, from the wheelhouse, came the stumbling, thudding sound of Old Judge Peterson and Philip Swanson tramping up from below. As they emerged through the wheelhouse door, Judge Peterson was leaning on Swanson with the finished fifth of Jack Daniels dangling from the crook of one finger. At the top of their lungs, the duo was singing:

"Rye whiskey! Rye whiskey! Rye whiskey, I cry! If you don't give me rye whiskey, I'll lay down and die—"

stopping mid-verse when Judge Peterson saw me and Sue Ann sitting side to side on the cooler.

"Well, well, well!" Judge Peterson bellowed. "Aren't you two a cozy pair?"

We sprang to our feet.

"It's not what you think!" I began to explain—

but never got to finish as the old man's body suddenly went limp.

Sue Ann and I came quickly to Swanson's assistance. Peterson had passed out in Swanson's arms. Just like that. I grabbed him by the legs while Sue Ann and Swanson got hold of his arms. We lugged is 250-plus frame to the skiff. There, we loaded him in—in much the same manner he'd been unloaded.

"You gonna be all right on the row back to the Mighty Mert?" Swanson asked, once Miss Sue Ann Bonnet had found her position at the oars. She had to sit herself down between Peterson's stilt-like legs, using his armpits as foot locks for her boots.

As they shoved off the Western World with an oar, Swanson called out:

"Hope George don't get no ideas about you two rowing off in the moonlight like this!"

"Don't get my hopes up!" Sue Ann called back.

Swanson and I watched as the skiff waddled farther and farther away, until the only way we knew the skiff was still out there was by the sound of oars still slapping the water. I thought it strange how Miss Sue Ann Bonnet hadn't said goodbye to me, hadn't even looked at me since Swanson and Peterson appeared.

"What were you two up to back here?" Swanson said, jabbing me in the ribs with a stiff finger.

"I don't know," I said.

I thought about telling him about the trees, and then thought better of it.

"She mentioned something about me reminding her of someone she knew a long time ago."

"Hmm," Swanson said. "That's probably it. You probably remind her of the fella' she knew when she was a young gal.

Engaged to the guy, I think. Indian—like her old man. Haida? No—Tlingit! Grew up on the Rez together. Anyway, this fella' went out on a crab boat one summer—but never came back. First time out. Judge Peterson said she went a little ding-dong after that. Got messed up in all that 60's hippie shit. Then on to Dutch Harbor where she worked as a stripper for a few years . . . until George came along and made an honest woman out of her. George treats her real nice—but I guess she still trips out from time to time."

"Course," Swanson added, stiff fingering me in the ribs again. "I've never been with Miss Sue Ann Bonnet when she was trippin'!"

Chapter Nine

Pelican, U.S.A.: Part One

It was almost ten before I arrived at the front steps of the Elbow Room in Pelican, Alaska. Because it was Saturday night, I was not the only one to think of taking a shower at Loretta's Laundry Shower Shack. I had to wait an hour for my turn to take "the plunge"—as the fisherman in front of referred to it:

"A buck-fifty a minute!" he said, rolling his bloodshot eyes at the cost. "And that ain't the worst of it. That buck-fifty hot shower lasts maybe thirty seconds—forty, if you're lucky. And, boy—when she stops, she stops ice cold. Hardly time enough to grab hold of your nuts and get out with what's left of your manhood!"

The Pelican evening was refreshingly clear. On the walk to the Elbow Room, varying shades of blue sky and bruised clouds scattering overhead reflected off the huge mirror-like puddles left after the day's showers. I waved back at several groups of cannery workers hosing off each other's rubber overalls at the end of their shifts. I stepped inside a telephone booth to call Brian Connelly back in Juneau, only to step back out self-consciously when I remembered I'd spent the last of my resources on a shave and shower.

I was greeted by the smell of stale, slopped beer as I stepped up on the Elbow Room's big front porch. Bluesy rock n' roll music wafted through the establishment's Western-Style swinging doors. Clusters of men and women had strayed out onto the porch to talk and take in these first and last rays of yellow sunshine. I was glad when I spotted no door guard. Since I was only eighteen, I was wondering if I'd even be able to get in.

Maneuvering past two drunk women—I saw—or thought I saw—Miss Sue Ann Bonnet at a far end of the porch.

"My, my, my!" the louder of the two women said, standing directly in front of me. "This one's just out of the bath! When'd you get off the boat, sailor?"

The women were dressed up like trick-riders at a rodeo: complete with chaps, Howdie-Doodie-style hats, even lassoes around their shoulders. They were obviously twins: same rob-in-egg eyes and frizzy Ronald McDonald red hair.

Out the corner of my eye, I saw Miss Sue Ann Bonnet standing by herself along the porch railing. She was gazing towards the water, smoking a cigarette. I was sure she was Sue Ann—or Sue Ann's twin sister: that same slender, slightly erect figure, same flowing, raven-colored hair, same fragile manner of bringing her smoke to her lips. Because her back was to me, I'd only seen her face for a half-second before another gust of wind blew her hair back across her face.

"This one's mine, Cheryl!" the second sister said. She'd snuck up from behind and dropped a lasso over me. Cinching the rope tight, she pulled me towards her.

"Hear that sailor!" she continued, in a mock serious tone. "Your ass is mine!"

Embarrassed, I laughed along with the sisters as they simultaneous kissed me on both cheeks.

"Wow!" I said. "Guess I came to the right place!"

Undoing the lasso, the sisters set me free: but not before I promised them a dance later on.

"Promise," I said.

The giggling sisters moved away from me, setting their sights on two more young fellows climbing the porch.

I'd lost sight of Sue Ann behind a moving wall of smiling, laughing Elbow Room patrons. I moved quickly now, feeling that I'd lost her. I wanted to speak with her here—alone—on the porch. Inside there would be all the others– including, maybe, probably, her husband, George. I kept bumping into people and repeatedly excusing myself. Then, just when I was ready to give up the ghost, I caught another glimpse of her. My heart pounding up somewhere near my throat, I shoved my way through the crowd. I imagined I could even smell her now—through all the smoke and beer—as I remembered the lavender-like smell of her that night on the boat when she sat beside me on the cooler. When I finally made it to that spot along the railing there was a woman there, but it was not Sue Ann Bonnet.

Actually, she was a young girl, Indian, about fourteen, maybe fifteen. She'd been absently twirling a rubber band— or hair band—something—around a finger. Apparently, my sudden appearance had either frightened or embarrassed her. Blushing, she began to walk away.

"Wait!" I said, my own face flushing. "I'm sorry. I thought you were someone else!"

She walked on. Frozen, I watched as she made her way along the railed walkway on one side of the whitewashed building. Twice she stopped to look back at me: like a frightened doe. The last time she stopped halfway to the back beside a screen door blown open by the wind. Her hair blew across the side of her face in the same way it had when I'd first mistaken her of Miss Sue Ann Bonnet. Another wall of men and women crossed in front of me, obscuring my view. When I was able to see down that railed walkway again . . . there was only that same stack of red and blue plastic milk crates and a few empty beer kegs lying on their sides.

The girl was gone.

"Long time no see!" Philip Swanson said, grabbing hold of my elbow.

I'd walked right by Swanson and Old Judge Peterson's booth. The inside of the Elbow Room was a mobbed with people as the porch. When Swanson caught up to me, I was just about to walk into a restroom marked SQUAWS in glaring-red neon overhead.

"Woops!" I said, shuffling out of the way of two women lurching between us into the restroom.

"What's that on your face?" Swanson asked, shouting over the zoo-like chatter and metallic glare of music coming from a jukebox.

"My face?" I said.

Swanson turned me towards some brass paneling on the wall so I could see my reflection. Two big lipstick smudges framed my cheeks: one a classic red, the other a hot pink.

"What the hell?"

I licked the back of my hand and did my best to rub away the rubbery smudges.

Swanson was doubled-up in hysterics. Grinning, I asked him what was so damn funny.

"Look around for yourself!"

At first, I did not notice a thing. There were so many people moving in and moving out. Then, I noticed. Young men, embarrassingly like myself, were entering through the Elbow Room's swinging doors, alone and in pairs, with the same glaring red and day-glo pink lipstick smudges on their cheeks.

"What's going on?" I said.

"Cheryl and Jeanine Rutter," Swanson said, his eyes still watery from laughing. "The sisters are branding every green-horn that crosses the Elbow Room's porch!"

Swanson handed me a can of Pabst Blue Ribbon beer.

"Come on!" he said. "Show's about to start!"

Swanson was a bobbing beacon I followed through the swirling crowd: his high-hitching shoulder and orangutan gait making his compact body swing side to side like a buoy on troubled seas. He seemed a different person amongst these strangers: a de-fanged version of his Pit Bull self. Whereas he usually tolerated my presence as one might a bothersome gnat, he was gracious, even fawning. We were sidekicks now!

The Elbow Room was enormous. The barn-sized room was divided by a short flight of steps so the rear half rested on a plane a yard lower than the front half. Behind the long, shuffleboard shaped counter, the liquor was stacked on shelves towards the ceiling so bartenders had to climb sliding ladders to get at particular bottles. Red stained-glass light fixtures and bladed ceiling fans were hung from the vaulted, onion-domed ceiling. At one time, Swanson told me, the Elbow Room Bar and Grill had been known as Saint Nicholas Russian Orthodox Church. Now, instead of crosses and rosaries and figurines of Madonna and child, the dark paneled walls were covered with posters of Seattle Seahawks football players and big-breasted blondes with wet T-shirts advertising beer and with taxidermies of everything from sea otters to bald eagles to King salmon—even a twenty-foot stuffed Orca fixed on a ledge over the swinging doors at the entrance. Instead of altars and prayer stalls, there were pool tables and big screen TVs.

The house lights dimmed as we descended a short flight of red-carpeted steps towards our booth. I'd been anxiously searching for Miss Sue Ann Bonnet: expecting her to come up and grab me any minute. Arriving at our small wooden booth, I thought I'd finally found her. I was disappointed when the shapely woman in the red T-shirt with long black hair turned out to be our cocktail waitress.

"Hey, there, Philly!" a man at our table called out– whistling between his fingers. "How's it going, bub? This your new boy?"

Four other men were at our booth besides Old Judge Peterson. I'd recognized them as fishermen the moment I saw the gnarled, tool-like quality of their hands. The tabletop was cluttered with their highball glasses, beer cans, and half-finished pitchers of beer. All four fishermen wore their flannel shirts buttoned at the wrist. The fisherman who had referred to me as "boy" was a wearing a DESERT STORM baseball cap and Ray-Ban sunglasses. The combination of the cap and the sunglasses and the man's pearly whites made me think of a walking talking skeleton. I'd disliked this man from the moment he whistled though his fingers.

"Yeah," Swanson said, taking a seat beside Judge Peterson. "Adam Porter."

"Adam, huh?" the man said. "Where you from, Adam?"

"Idaho," I said, squeezing myself into the tight-fitting booth.

"Idaho!" the man repeated. "That's God's country!"

And Reverend Butler's. . . I thought.

Old Judge Peterson was getting up from his side of the booth now.

"Going, Judge?" I asked.

Peterson looked older, more tired than I remembered. Age spots showed on his big boney hands and face. His jaw and nose seemed more prominent: like a salmon's during its spawning stage. When we'd arrived, he actually been dozing off, his big chin on his chest. He stumbled as he climbed out of the booth, tripping over a leg of a chair. He might have hit the floor if Swanson and I hadn't grabbed hold of him.

"Steady, Judge," I said. "We got you."

Elbows flying, Peterson shook himself loose of our grasp.

"Let me be!" he said. "I still got two good legs!"

Winking at me, Swanson asked Peterson if he wouldn't stay for a quick one.

Peterson hesitated, his horny brow frowning over like a turtle's; then, literally shaking himself out of it, he staunchly announced:

"Nope. Nope. Got to be going. George wants to put-out for Esther Island tonight—on account of this new closure coming up. And I promised Sue Ann I'd be back for supper an hour ago."

As Peterson walked away, the man in the DESERT STORM cap called out:

"Be sure to give Sue Ann a big hello from me! Hey, Judge!"

He had a toothpick in the craw of his mouth now and was chewing on it as though a stick of gum. Watching Peterson balk, then shrug his shoulders and walk on, I wanted to sock the bastard. Shove his toothpick down his hole. Toss beer in his face. Something.

"No," Swanson said, under his breath as we sat down again. "Ignore the bastard. He's drunk. . ."

"What an asshole!" I mumbled back. "Someone should teach—"

Our conversation was cut short by the loud squelch of a microphone.

'TESTING . . . TESTING . . . ONE, TWO—"a man's voice boomed of the P.A. system. "TESTING . . . ONE, TWO, THREE, FOUR . . . SUZIE AND SALLY STETCHED OUT ON THE FLOOR. . ."

I located the man with the microphone: a big Indian guy standing center-stage on a small bandstand along the rear wall. He was dressed in jeans and a black Jack Daniel's T-shirt. The T-shirt was two sizes too small for him so his gut bulged out the bottom of it.

"What's going on?" I said.

"Sssh!" Swanson said, handing me a glass of beer from our table. "Watch!"

Men and women were jockeying for position around the railing of what appeared to be sunken dance floor below the bandstand. Some of the revelers were carrying quart-sized bottles of beer. They looped their arms over each other's shoulders and backsides and seemed to be having as much fun jockeying for position as they were viewing the spectacle below.

Swanson and I and our whole table got up and stood at the edge of the circle growing around the dance floor. Swanson introduced me to the Rapp brothers—Tom and Hank—from Wrangell, Alaska. The one with the DESERT STORM cap and sunglasses went by the name of Waters. The fourth fisherman was Maxwell Jones, a friend of Waters whom Swanson had never met before.

"Steer clear of Waters," Swanson warned me. "He's way out of your league, kid. Ex-Navy Seal. Panama. Grenada. He'll be knocking at your door. Already is. Just let him keep knocking. . ."

We followed the four other fishermen forward. Behind weaving heads and shoulders came glimpses of the sunken dance floor. It had been turned into a huge mud trough. A man dressed as a clown in a referee's outfit was leveling the red clay mud with a rake. The M.C. had climbed down from the bandstand and was whispering in the ear of one of the two women in bikini bathing suits. Along a far wall, an oilcloth banner proclaimed LADIES MUD WRESTLING NIGHT!!! I wondered why I hadn't noticed it before.

"Ever been to a wrestle before?"

I shook my head, thinking Swanson had asked the question. Turning my eyes from the woman in the thong, I saw that one of the Rapp brothers had asked the question: the younger, stouter one, Tom Rapp.

"Then you're in for some fun tonight, young Adam!" Tom Rapp said, looping a thick forearm around my neck. "Woo wee! Mud-wrestle, Alaska-style!"

The silver casing round his left front tooth gleamed under the bandstand lights.

"Just stick by me, Adam," he continued. "Things can get a little outta hand sometimes . . . but we'll pull you through!"

"Outta hand?" I said. "Whatya' mean a little outta hand? Tom Rapp only laughed. Pulling a metal flask out from his back pocket, he yelled:

"Here . . . take a slug of this."

I took a swallow, choking, of course.

"What the hell's in there?" I managed to croak out.

"Wild Turkey!" he said, taking a nip himself.

The M.C. was speaking over the P.A. again. But it was impossible to make out his words above the whistling and catcalls. Tom Rapp and I moved forward with the throng. We were soon cut off from the rest of our party. I saw Water's

DESERT STORM cap bobbing above the mob, and then it too was blotted from view by the swarming patrons.

Suddenly, from somewhere across the room, a laser fixed on a mirrored-ball hanging over the trough. White and green spinning dots of light were refracted around the bar—sliding off of the faces, hands and clothes of all those around so the Elbow Room seemed to be shifting on its rudder. A man—or woman?—kept stumbling into me from behind and was repeatedly excusing him—or her?—self. We were packed so tight it was next to impossible to turn around.

The wrestlers entered the trough. One was a blonde, the other a brunette. They had very shapely figures: like those women you see advertising exercise equipment on TV. Their faces were rouged and powdered; their hair tied back in ponytails. The one in the thong bathing suit—the blonde—had the Big Dipper constellation tattooed on her ass. This was the symbol of the Alaska state flag—and I learned later from Swanson—the symbol of the Alaska secession from the Union movement.

"Here we go!" Tom Rapp yelled—as we lurched forward. "Mama! Get a load of the view!"

He passed me the flask. I took a long swallow, not choking this time.

The clown in the referee garb had the women clasp hands. He blew his whistle and the match began. The women circled each other, thumping their chests, clawing the air, stamping their shanks about in the mud like mountain goats trying to find footing on a rocky precipice. Big-time wrestling stuff. Within seconds, they were in a hold. Seconds later, the first of the women's tops came off.

The crowd was ecstatic. The wrestler with the Big Dipper tattoo paraded her opponent's bikini top overhead like a scalp.

On cue from the M.C., the referee jumped in and called an end to round one. I had seen enough. I was feeling suffocated and wanted to leave—but the crowd was worse now than ever. Men and women were literally crawling over one another's shoulders and heads to see into the trough. Little skirmishes were flaring up: one man holding a hand over his bleeding nose and yelling two feet from my right ear drum. Those of us who had been in the front rows were pressed against the railing now. Some of us, like Tom Rapp, were hanging at ninety-degree angles out over the trough. Others, such as me, were pushing back at the sheer wall of people pressing us forward like rugby players in a scrum.

The thing I feared most happened as round two of the mud-wrestle began. While the brunette was dragging the blonde though the mud by the hair . . . flaunting her mud-caked breasts . . . the railing finally gave way. It had been tottering for some time now and, as it busted forward, it sent half the crowd (and yours truly) toppling into the mud along with it.

Next thing I knew I was face down in the trough—choking and sputtering on a mouthful of mud. Others piled on top of me. I tried to remain calm, but soon found myself punching and kicking and screaming along with the rest of them when an unseen hand pinched fiercely on the back of my leg—refusing to let go.

Eventually, we began to untangle. Arms, legs, heads and bodies had gotten so entangled and covered in slop that it was hard to tell who's what was connected to who's body. Twice I felt I'd come close to suffocating. When Tom Rapp helped me up, I clung to him out of sheer gratitude.

"Was that normal?" I said, gasping for breath like a fish out of water.

The house lights were turned up to a glaring level now. The wrestlers and their ringmasters were nowhere to be seen.

"Hell, yes!" Tom Rapp said—positively beaming. "Mud-wrestle, Alaska-style!"

I smiled back in disbelief.

Not only was Tom Rapp knee deep in mud, he was completely blackfaced—dripping with the goop.

"Your face!" I said.

The silver casing from his left front tooth shined like the North Star under the bright lights. Tom leaned heavily against me and, winking, said,

"Take a look at your own mug, kid!"

After washing what I could out of my hair and off my skin and clothes with bar towels and paper napkins, I returned to the new site of our party thinking things couldn't get any weirder or wilder than this.

They would.

Swanson and the others had joined up with a larger party at a cafeteria-sized table towards the front of the Elbow Room. Swanson was engaged in heated discussion with Waters at the other end of the table and had not acknowledged my hello when I sat down between Tom and Hank Rapp.

Many of the patrons were leaving. Those us who remained seemed bent on making up for this loss of energy by consolidating forces at this one long table. The top of it was so cluttered with beer glasses that many of us began drinking straight from the pitchers. Dollar bills and cigarettes were so scattered—and went through so many hands as one person borrowed from another and was, likewise, borrowed from—that no one seemed to mind when someone across the table slid a ten-dollar bill out from beneath their neighbor's glass or borrowed a few cigarettes without asking. The party was in such high gear, in fact, that many of the women were already seated in the men's laps. Within moments of taking my own seat, one was in mine.

I'd been saluting Tom and Hank Rapp with a full pint when the woman appeared.

"Grrr-owll!" the woman said, lacing arms and fingers around my neck and shoulders—actually purring into my ear like Cat-Woman in the old Batman TV series. "If you ain't one handsome son of a bitch!"

In her enthusiasm, she'd knocked my beer glass out of my hand, spilling some on both of us. When I reached down to pick up the glass, she grabbed my wrist and placed a fresh one in my hand.

"Never mind, silly,' she said, smiling, pouring beer into it so I had to hold it perfectly still in fear she'd dump more on us. "There's plenty more where that came from!"

"Thanks. . ."

"Helen," she said, picking up on my cue.

I'd be a liar if I said I wasn't attracted to this woman. There was definitely something about her smoky gray eyes and the way she bit her lower lip as she looked me over.

"Look it here, Shirley," she said to the heavy-set redhead in Hank Rapp's lap. "Doesn't he remind you of that actor, Jon Voight—in that movie with Jane Fonda—COMING HOME?" Running her fingertip down the length of my nose, she whispered, just to me:

"He was so goddamn sexy in that wheelchair I wanted to climb right up on that silver screen and jump his bones!"

Although I hadn't seen the movie—had never even heard of the actor at that time—I was not so naïve to not fully understand the import of her words. Overwhelmed, I began to pour more beer into our glasses—slopping it, of course, on both our laps.

"Oh, you devil!" Helen giggled. "Now look what you've done!"

"Sorry!" I said. "I guess I've had too much—"

Stopping when, Helen, sponging my beer-soaked lap with a wad of table napkins, kissed me full on the mouth.

I did not resist.

"Whoa, there! Whoa!" I heard someone saying—their voice a long way off.

Figuring it was probably just my conscience, I went on doing what it was I was doing with Helen when I heard the voice again—this time, with my name attached.

"Adam! Heel! Down, boy! Earth calling Adam. . ."

It was Hank Rapp. Straightening, I asked the older Rapp brother what was wrong.

"Nothing's wrong," Hank Rapp said, winking at the redhead in his lap. "Nothing at all."

Obviously, they were sizing Helen and me up for something. Looking to Helen for a cue, she averted eye contact by feigning interest in buttoning the top buttons of my shirt. Finally, Hank Rapp said:

"You like Helen?"

"Like Helen?" I repeated, thinking things were definitely getting weirder—by the second.

"What I'm trying to say, "Hank Rapp said, holding a finger to the side of his lips so the redhead would stop her giggling. "Is do you or don't you like Helen? 'Cuz if you do, we're heading over to Roxie's Kitchen. All of us. Me and Tom, Fred Waters and Maxwell Jones . . . and the girls, of course. You're welcome to come along. I already talked to Phil about it and he says it's all right by him if it's all right by you . . . that he'll take care of it. He said he'll probably meet us there himself as soon as he gets back from the boat."

"Back from the boat?" I repeated.

I glanced down the other end of the table and saw another man sitting in Swanson's spot beneath the bladed ceiling fan.

Noticing that the whole table was watching me, it finally dawned on me. Helen was a whore. Of course—how stupid of me! How vain to think just any woman would come walking up out of nowhere and throw herself upon me! How else explain a scene like this: all these men and women in each other's laps like something out of an episode of GUNSMOKE or THE WILD, WILD WEST? Glancing towards Tom Rapp, he raised his eyebrow as if to indicate:

"Yep. Whores. . ."

"Well," Hank Rapp said, getting a little test. "What's it going to be, son?"

"Sure," I heard myself saying. "If Helen doesn't mind."

Everyone, with the exception of Helen and me, busted out laughing.

I bristled—especially at the sound of Fred Waters repeating what I'd said at the other end of the table.

"Atta, boy!" Hank Rapp said, slapping me hard between the shoulder blades. "Good man!"

Helen kissed me full on the mouth.

Across the table, Tom Rapp was already standing.

"To Roxie's!" Tom Rapp shouted, thumping the bottom of his glass on the table.

"Roxie's! Roxie's! Roxie's!" the others shouted back.

Chapter Ten

Pelican, U.S.A.: Part Two

ALASKA: A map of it outlined in day-glo spray paint on the big metal door at the back of Roxie's Kitchen.

It was dark out and pouring down rain when our party from the Elbow Room stepped out. The establishment was closing as we left: one of the bartenders coming out on the porch after us to draw the storm shudders across the Elbow Room's big bay windows. In the short time I'd been inside, an offshore storm had hit Pelican—blackening the skies. Lights around the village were either out or threatening to go out because of the winds. The windows of the closed down shacks and stores were black and speckled with rain. I saw a tugboat towing a supply barge up to one of the terminals below . . . the deck lights from the tug seeming a long way off because of the swirling sheets of rain.

I held Helen against my side. Our little party had bunched together, singing vulgarized versions of a half-dozen songs nobody knew all the lyrics to. Tom Rapp was telling a wild story of Alaskan brown bears in Barrow, Alaska who got so drunk on rotting fermented berries in the fall that when you roamed the downtown streets of Barrow at night you had to watch out you didn't get in a tussle with a goddamn bear!

When we arrived at Roxie's Kitchen, we discovered the front door was locked, and a sign in the window that the kitchen was closed. Of course, there were two stories to this brick building. Lights were on in the windows of some of the rooms above the café. Figures were moving behind the closed red curtains. The big neon sign over the front door was still on. Its red letters hissed and sputtered back at the pelts of rain. Tom Rapp had noticed that the two bulbs at the end of the sign were flickering so it read "Roxie's Kitch—"instead of Roxie's Kitchen. Tom found this hilarious and kept shouting:

"Roxie's Kitch–! Roxie's Kitch–!"

as we hurried down a narrow walkway to the back door of the building.

There, we stumbled upon some Indians, about a half-dozen of them. They'd been huddled beneath the outer stair-well (leading to the rooms above the café), passing around a bottle of Mad Dog 20/20 wine, trying to stay dry. As we approached, they came out from their cover to panhandle for money and cigarettes.

ALASKA: A map of it spray-painted on the service door for the café directly behind the stairs. There was a caption written within the map, but I had not been able to decipher it. I could read it plain enough now:

"WHITE ALASKA SUCKS!"

The rain had slowed to a drizzle, making things oddly quiet. The alley was lit up by a single lamp at the top of the stairs. The appearance of the Indians set-off members of our party.

"The natives look restless tonight, gents!" Maxwell Jones joked.

If I had learned anything by now, it was that out here on the "fringes", people were a little plainer with each other than in "polite" society. Moreover, no one really gave a fuck what you thought of them, because, if you had any lick of sense at all, then why the fuck were you there with them in the first place?

Hank Rapp shoved one of the panhandlers backwards into a 50-gallon grease barrel—knocking down both the barrel and panhandler. Laughter replaced the curses and sneers at the slapstick sight of the intoxicated Indian trying to stand back up with the barrel rolling into him each time he moved. All the dirty cooking grease the dishwasher poured into the barrel at closing time was streaming out across the gravel lot. Tears of laughter came when the Indian managed to stand, covered from head to foot with the grease.

In spite of this, the Indian continued to panhandle in sloth-like deliberation. I also knew enough to know if these Indians didn't let-up . . . and soon . . . there would be trouble.

"Hey, Tonto! You and the tribe move along. This is our Holy Ground now Chief!"

It was Waters. He wasn't wearing his sunglasses now, but still had on the DESERT STORM cap and still had a toothpick in his trap. I remembered the warning Swanson had given me about Waters.

The big Indian threw the first blow: a wheelhouse left. Waters easily slipped the punch—stepping to his right and following with two quick jabs and an undercut right that dropped his opponent to the ground. Our party cheered: minus me. Waters smiled big, shaking his right hand to show that it stung a little from the punch. He still had the toothpick in his mouth.

Our party roared at the sight of the big Indian standing up behind Waters. I noticed that he more tottered than stood: leaning forward like a tree cut to fall. He lowered his head and charged the still smiling Waters. Like a matador sidestepping a bull, Waters used the Indian's own momentum against him. At the last instant, Waters faced his charging opponent, stepped to the left and guided him into the brick wall behind them with a little underhanded push. The Indian hit the wall full force: crumpling instantly.

It was now I joined the fight. With the Indian sprawled at his feet, Waters had placed his steel-toed boot on the man's face and begun to press down. Shaking loose of Helen's hold, I charged forward and blindsided Waters on his ass.

Scrambling to his feet, Waters lunged towards me, but was held back by Hank Rapp and Maxwell Jones. Tom Rapp stood between us both.

"Hold it!" Rapp shouted—above Water's accusations I was a faggot and an ass-licking Indian lover and my accusation he was a Nazi and a coward. "Both of you! Right now! Cool it, for Christ's sake. . ."

I stepped back, my head whirling. Everything had happened so fast. Waters had worked over the big Indian like a machine on an assembly like stamping out one product amongst a thousand.

Hank Rapp and Maxwell Jones released Waters now. I braced for a charge, but Waters appeared played out. He accepted his DESERT STORM cap back from one of the women and shoved it on his head. He was still cursing and glaring at me—but definitely calmed down.

The big Indian was moving now. The right side of his face was streaked with rain, gravel and blood. He right eye was already swollen shut, the left eye on the way there. But he was moving. His friends helped him to his feet. He did not decline a swallow from the bottle of wine.

Helen, noticing my concern, stepped closer.

"See. . ." she said, brushing up against my arm. "Charley's all right. He gets in scraps like this all the time. An hour from now he'll be telling the whole town he won the fight. Take my word for it. Tomorrow he'll go to the village clinic, if he wants. For nothing. He's an Indian."

The rest of our party had already climbed the stairs to the second level. One of the women called back:

"Hurry up, Helen. Big Al says he's gonna lock the doors if ya' don't hurry. Tell the kid to make up his mind."

I shivered from the cold. I could beat it back to the boat right now. Get out of this rain. Get out of this whole mess.

"Come on, honey," Helen said, brushing against me again. "Can't you see it's raining?"

I underdressed alone in the room Helen had directed me to. She would join me presently.

I trembled as I climbed out of my rain-soaked clothing: not so much from the chill of the room as from the realization I was in an actual house of prostitution. I spread my jeans over the room's hot water radiator to dry. After spending days and nights on end in clothes—stinky itchy greasy clothes—it felt wonderful to simply be naked. The feel of the cush, rose-patterned carpet under my bare feet was almost decadent.

The rest of our party had found their way to their own rooms before Helen and I entered the lobby. The lobby consisted of two dilapidated love seats set at right angles, a scratched-up coffee table and two lamps with ruffled-lacing around their shades. The paneled walls were stripped bare: just a few shreds of old calendars still clinging to the walls' staples. Two men I'd never seen before were seated on one of the love seats, distractedly fingering through porn magazines they'd picked out from a large stack spread across the coffee table. Both smiled at Helen—winking at her, referring to her by name. Helen had ruefully ignored them and signaled me to do likewise, whispering in my ear:

"Cannery dinks."

She'd run the back of her hand across her lips as though having spoken the words had produced a foul scum there.

Before I'd been able to take a second look at them, Helen had shoved me on ahead: room No. 8 at the end of the long dark hallway.

The layout of the room reminded me of the one I'd seen at the Ivory Inn in Elfin Cove: the same double bed, same matching urinal and washbasin, same mirrored-ceiling over the bed. What struck me as different was the in-use quality of the place. The bed sheets were torn from their stays, tumbling towards the floor. The bed-frame was set at a crooked angle, as though having been pushed away from the wall. On the night stand beside the bed was a half-finished drink in a plastic throwaway cup (ice cubes not yet melted) and beside that, in an ashtray, the stub of a half-finished cigarette.

A bottle of Broker's whiskey was on a little table beside the window. Figuring it part of the package deal, I poured myself a drink in one of the plastic cups. I peeled back the burlap curtains to get a peek at the storm. Because the window was cracked open and was directly above the red neon restaurant sign outside, I could hear the rain hiss and sputter on the bulbs below.

The truth is I was having second thoughts (that is, if a man standing buck-naked in a whorehouse is even capable of having second thoughts . . . let alone true ones). What the hell was I doing here? And where was this damn Helen anyway? Had she doubled-back to do a number on those "cannery dinks" in the lobby? The idea of her spreading her legs for these men and, a minute later, coming in to do the same for me was detestable.

I poured myself a second drink.

For some crazy reason, I thought of the time Peggy Alexander and I made love in the backseat of her '69 Buick Skylark the summer before my senior year of high school. What I member most about Peggy was not so much her strawberry blonde hair and long beautiful Amazon legs but her Great Dane dog—Duchess.

Duchess was with Peggy Alexander wherever she went. Wherever. She had been there the first time Peggy and I actually made love. That summer, during intermission at the Blue-Ox Drive In, we'd traded places with the dog—shoving Duchess in the front seat while we scampered into the back seat. I'd even bought the hound a couple of hot dogs as a kind of peace offering. About ten minutes in the second feature, only moments after I'd entered Peggy Alexander for the first time—after God knows how many false starts—what happens but the dog shits herself in the front seat of the Buick. Now, of course . . . at the time of this discourtesy. .. Peggy and I had went right on making love. . .I thinking that that sound and the odor had escaped from her body. . .and Peggy thinking it had from mine. What a surprise we had a few minutes later when, finally looking into the front seat, we saw Duchess burying her head under the dashboard in shame.

Now that was a good old-fashioned roll in the hay! What I was scheduled for here was to take part in a stinking business transaction. Where was the abandon? the innocence? the fun?

"Fuck it. . ." I heard myself say out loud.

I didn't need this shit. I was a free man! I'd tip-toe out the exit door here at the end of the hall. . .or if it was locked. . .just march right through the lobby with head held high. . .just go ahead and try to stop me now. They didn't know me from Adam. Probably wouldn't even notice my absence. Next number please. . .

There were three soft taps on the door.

"Shit. . ." I mumbled aloud, grabbing my jeans.

My eyes fixed on the enamel-spotted doorknob. When nothing happened—at first—I wondered if I'd only imagined this tapping. Maybe the sounds came from the rooms next door? A second later, though, the doorknob turned over and the door opened.

Expecting to see Helen, instead a maid's cleaning cart rumbled into the room, followed by a young girl pushing the cart directly towards the bed.

Silently, I cursed at the girl. Although her back was turned to me as she fitted the first clean sheet over the bed, and though I'd only caught a glimpse of the side of her face, I had a funny feeling I'd seen her before. Hoping to dress before she spotted me, I continued to struggle into my damp jeans. Unfortunately, while keeping one eye on her slim backside and another on the jeans I was hurriedly crawling into . . . I suddenly noticed, with the other eye now, that I'd climbed into my jeans backwards. Feeling it would be infinitely more ridiculous to be caught with my pants on backwards than with no pants at all, I reversed the process with the same haste. Only now, instead of keeping one eye trained on the girl and the other on my jeans, I fixed both eyes on the task tangled around my ankles. What happened next I would never quite figure out? Whether as a result of this sudden change of focus (from a balanced one-eye up/one-eye down to the more lopsided both eyes down) or because the big toe on my left foot had caught on the fly of my jeans . . . next thing I knew I was face down on the floor . . . my jeans twisted horribly around my ankles . . . ass straight up in the air.

While struggling to right myself, I saw the cleaning maid slumped out on the floor beside the half-made bed. Her body was stricken with strange shakings and convulsions. Her mouth was wide open—as though to laugh—but produced low guttural choking sounds instead. Standing, I tugged my jeans to my waist and, leaving the fly undone, rushed to the girl's assistance. Lifting her from the floor to the bed, I soon discovered that what I had feared was a seizure or stroke was, in reality, a bizarre kind of laughter.

I also discovered, as I brushed back the hair from the girl's smiling, tear-soaked face, that she was, in fact, the very same young girl I'd mistaken for Miss Sue Ann Bonnet earlier this evening on the Elbow Room's porch.

"Excuse me," I began, standing up from the bed. "But aren't you—"

I stopped speaking as the girl became stricken with another streak of her bizarre laughter. Looking anxiously around the room for a probable cause . . . it wasn't until I'd given up the search and had, matter-of-factly, gazed down at my own person that I located the source of the girl's guffaws. My jeans had slipped down to my ankles again! Realizing how ridiculous I must have looked inquiring of her identity in so formal a fashion with my shlong dangling out there right in front of her, I was overcome with an attack of the first genuine out-and-out laughter I'd experienced since arriving in Alaska.

The girl had slid down the side of the bed again. I didn't even bother to raise her. Instead, I placed a comradely hand on one of her shoulders while she sat sprawled at me feet. And it was while in this seemingly obvious position Helen walked in on the girl and me.

"Tell him to hold his horses!" I heard Helen say as she appeared in the doorway. "Tell him to hold it till I get there."

Helen had been talking with someone down the hall and smiling when she first looked in on the spectacle of me and the cleaning girl and me laughing away at the foot of the unmade bed. Her smiling ceased as she entered the room.

"Well I'll be!" Helen exclaimed, hands on her hips. "If I ain't seen it all now!"

Helen had shed her old clothing and appeared now in a skintight blue leotard. Her gray eyes were smoking, and it was obvious she was just as pissed at me as she was with the girl. In spite of her 5'3" height, her thick chest and shoulders, and fiery disposition, made her surprisingly intimidating: like Jane Fonda on steroids.

While I finished buttoning my fly, Helen moved across the room in three lightning steps. Jerking the cleaning girl up off the floor, she backhanded her across the mouth so fiercely that the girl began to bleed instantly. Not allowing the girl to crumble just yet, Helen backhanded her across the other side of her face, letting her collapse this time.

"Goddamn deaf and dumb little wench! Working one of my Johns! If I ever—"

But Helen was unable to finish as I shoved her out in the hall.

"Lay off her!" I shouted. "She hasn't done a damn thing—"

I stopped when Helen went flying down the hall, yelling for help.

Furious, I knelt beside the girl with a towel I'd grabbed from her cleaning cart. I raised her to seated position against the doorjamb, my hands shaking as I pressed the towel to her mouth. Helen had referred to her as DEAF AND DUMB. DEAF AND DUMB! That was it! That is why the girl had appeared so strange there on the Elbow Room porch and why she appeared so strange now: her child-like body convulsing again; her mouth wide open—making the same guttural choking noises—tears once again streaming from her eyes—but not from laughter this time. From pain! Pain because she'd been mistaken for doing what Helen had been about to do to me. Tears filled my own eyes. I remembered how Sue Ann had told me that Alaska was not a whore . . . not something to hump and dump on. And here I was, only a few days later, literally doing the very same! But—NO!—not doing so! Saved by this strange angel!

"There he is! With the little wench!" I heard Helen shriek from down the hall.

Helen and two football-player sized men stomped up the hall towards us.

Resting the girl against the jamb, I stepped out in the hall to meet them. Surprising even myself, I caught the biggest of the two—the older one with the balding crew cut Helen had referred to as "Al"—right on the chin, bringing the man to the floor with a loud thud. My luck ran out with the second bouncer. Even though half-dressed men and women were flying out of their rooms to see what all the commotion was and thereby creating more commotion . . . and even though I was able to knock the wind out of the second bouncer while a brave boxer-shorts clad Tom Rapp held the man's arms back for me . . . I could not, would not, survive Helen:

Unbeknownst to me, Helen had tiptoed up from behind with a large porcelain vase and brought it down on top of my head.

Before completely blacking out, staring at the shards of vase around my skull, I heard the second bouncer say:

"Ah, Helen! He was a scrappy one. Why you always gotta go ruining things?"

And heard (or thought I heard) Helen reply:

"Shut up, Mac! Just get this lunk and the others he came in with outta here! We got customers to attend to!"

Chapter Eleven

Exchange at Sea

When I opened my eyes that morning. . .it wasn't to the image of Miss Sue Ann Bonnet spooning chicken broth into my mouth and replacing cold compresses from my forehead. . .as I'd been dreaming. . .rather. . .to Philip Swanson's upside-down face beaming down at me like Satan himself. . .kicking madly on the head-piece of my bed board inches from my left ear. . .yelling:

"Out of that bunk and up on deck! That's it! By God . . . look at him, boys. The Wonder kid from Roxie's Whorehouse! Out the night before to make it with all whorehouse employees and kick ass on every rebel-rouser and sorry son of a bitch in Pelican, U.S.A.! That's him all right. Rested now and just a-raring to go at them lines out back!"

"All right! All right!" I protested when Swanson started to physically pull me off the bed board. "I'm getting up—damn it!"

I swung my legs over the edge of the bed board. Thus, semi-seated, with my sleeping bag still wrapped around my legs, I was at least allowed to hold my head in my hands and wonder.

"What time is it? Where are we?"

There was enough light in the hull that I guessed it was somewhere around nine in the morning. I could tell by the familiar seesawing action of the floor that we were at sea, but this seesawing was more marked than usual.

Swanson had thrown together a pot of coffee and was lighting the stove's pilot.

"You slept through half the morning," Swanson said, extinguishing the match just before its flame reached his fingertips. Only Swanson had mastered the technique of lighting our damper less stove with a single matchstick. "After the Rapp brothers brought you down from Roxie's I let you sleep the rest of the way out."

I shook my head carefully. I remembered something about being carried back to the boat from the whorehouse and how Helen had dropped a vase over my head. Palming the top of my skull, I felt a bump the size of large walnut.

"Thanks. . ." I said. Then, checking myself for other bruises, added: "Where are we? How come we aren't in Pelican?"

Swanson explained that the Alaska Board of Fisheries out of Anchorage had posted an EMERGENCY THREE DAY CLOSURE coming up in three days. The bad thing about this was the dates of this closure coincided with the peak of the King Salmon Run. Each year, a day either way of a fixed calendar date, the greatest number of migrating King salmon flooded these inlet waters on way to their natal streams. The money made during these three days often determined a good season from a bad one. It was Swanson's opinion that the regulators had chosen to announce this closure date at the last minute to catch fishermen off guard.

This is why we'd put-out from Pelican last night for Esther Island. Esther Island was a misnomer: a kind of underwater reef that formed a shallow expanse of water salmon liked to travel over as they come off the open ocean. It was at the northern head of Chicagof Island, midway between Cross Sound and the Pacific Ocean. It was here Swanson believed we might "head-off" some of these salmon before they poured into the inlet waters from the open sea.

I remembered the conversation I'd had with Sue Ann Bonnet about decreasing fish counts and over fishing, but decided it was probably not a good idea to bring this up right now (particularly in wake of the trouble I'd caused the night before!).

"And that's where we are right now?" I said, my aching head beginning to throb.

"You got it!" said Swanson. Then, pouring himself a fresh cup of coffee, finished:

"I'd best get back the wheel. We're near a good-sized wash-rock 'bout now. Feel free to mug up . . . splash your face . . . and what-have-you. But don't be pussyfooting around. A little something's come up and I'm in need of your services above."

And like a bee ordered back to its hive, Swanson turned and disappeared up the 5-step ladder.

Dashing, tripping, stumbling, falling, crawling across the floor of the hull, I made it just in time to vomit into an empty herring bucket across the room. Like a dog over its dish, I held my face over the salt-rimmed bucket and continued to wretch. My skull squeezed down on my brain each time a new heave came up. In midst of this came a weird urge to pray. But to what God or image I could not think! Perhaps for the first time since I'd been out here I realized just how removed from the rest of the world I really was. No one, not even Brian Connelly back in Juneau, really knew where I was at this moment. I'd made reference in a post card that I was fishing: but as to exactly where and with whom I was fishing, nothing. As far as he or anyone else was concerned, I could be anywhere along the Alaskan coast from Ketchikan to the Bering Sea! Overwhelmed by the thought, I clawed the hardwood floor as a new wave of nausea rose up inside me.

Finally, there was an end to it—or, at least, a great slowing down. The spinning slowed. The hot flashes cooled. Slowly, very slowly, I stood up.

"Christ. . ." I thought aloud. "What have I gotten myself into?"

From above came the rattling interruption of Swanson's voice:

"Haul ass, down there! I need you on the bow-point! Pronto!"

"Screw yourself!" I cursed beneath my breath, knowing Swanson couldn't hear because of the engine.

Because the swells outside were getting worse, I opted to sit on the floor while getting dressed—one sock, one foot at a time.

"Right on time!" was the first thing Swanson said when I appeared on deck.

I'd found the wheelhouse deserted, and came upon Swanson taking a leak over leeward side.

The light outside and the sound of the Western's engine was brighter and louder than I'd even expected. The waters around us were bluer, wider than usual, choppier too. The boat was tacking hard right, as though caught in some strange whirlpool of a current. Not more than a hundred yards to the left of our wake, a capsized rowboat bobbed in a strange circular fashion on the water: like the dial on a broken compass.

"On time for what?" I said, looking away as Swanson adjusted himself in front of me.

Swanson pointed directly over my shoulder.

Turning to see, I saw nothing: just the wide-open swells rolling by, a few seagulls cartwheeling overhead. Shrugging my shoulders, I indicated that I didn't understand.

"No," Swanson said, once again pointing over my shoulder. "Up along the prow. Over the roof of the wheelhouse."

Still shaking my head, I stepped back a little and the object Swanson had so ardently been alluding to came into full and sudden view.

"H-o-l-y shit!" was the only thing I could think to say. "H-o-l-y fucking shit!"

No less than twenty feet off our prow, another trawler, the Lacey J, was running alongside us. Two men in stocking caps on the Lacey J's deck were waving good- naturedly at us. With a shudder, I noticed that no one was at the wheel of the Lacey J. And there was no one at our wheel either! Had this positioning taken place in a quiet harbor or cove, I'd think little of it. But here—on a flooding sea, in some of the roughest water I'd encountered yet—the closeness of the other vessel was terrifying.

"Look at those crack-heads!" I said, turning my torso towards Swanson but unable to turn my eyes from the Lacey J in irrational fear that doing so might cause our two trawlers to collide. "What are they up to? They must be twelve-miles high!"

Braving a glance in Swanson's direction, I discovered I'd been talking to a steel pipe.

"SWANSON!"

The wheelhouse! I thought. Of course! Swanson had gone there to steer us clear of these two fools and their trawler!

But entering the wheelhouse, I found it as vacant as when I'd first come up. The steering wheel was locked in auto-pilot: turning a quarter turn to the right, thumping to a stop, bouncing back to the left, and then repeating the process.

Rushing back outside, I searched fore and aft for my skipper. After stumbling over a toolbox and saving myself from toppling overboard by grabbing a steel cable, a horrid thought entered my brain. Maybe Swanson had fallen overboard. The way the boat was rocking and wind was blowing it wouldn't take much to toss anyone, even an old salt like Swanson. Swayed by this notion, I scrambled about on deck in renewed hysteria.

Not until I'd literally tripped over Swanson did I uncover the secret of his whereabouts.

"Hey! Aaaaah! Get off–!"

While searching out to sea for Swanson's floating carcass, I'd inadvertently stepped on his outstretched hands just as he was climbing up from the holds below deck.

A strong swell rocked the Western World's stern, forcing Swanson to grasp my leg as he crawled up out of the hatchway. I grabbed his elbow and lifted him to his feet.

"Thanks. . ." Swanson grumbled, then quickly added:

"Here. Take this. Like this!"

Swanson shoved a half-frozen salmon into my arms.

Shocked, I simply stared at the fish.

Swanson grabbed my stiff hands and twisted them about until I was holding the fish properly through their gills.

"That's better," he said. "It's a fish. Not a goddamn infant!"

The Lacey J's position had slid back so it was riding left to our stern. Only one of the crewmembers was on deck now, the other manning the wheel.

"Yo! Swanson!" the stocking-capped man at the rear of the Lacey J called across the white-capped waters. "We ain't got all morning."

Swanson shrugged his shoulders and nodded towards me.

"Yeah, well. . ." the other fisherman answered. "We still ain't got all day."

Swanson gave a big thumb's up sign to his fellow fisherman. Under his breath, he mumbled to me:

"What a doofus! Word is his pretty young wife is banging some cannery hand while he's out here busting his balls!"

I noticed the stocking-capped fisherman was no longer smiling and was leaning over the side of the Lacey J as if to hear what Swanson was saying.

"Come on," Swanson said, nudging me forward. "You heard the man. We need your services on the bow. Pronto!"

"The bow?" I asked. "In these waters? How come?"

We were at the door of the wheelhouse now. Inside, scattered electric messages sounded on and off over the CB radio. Through the water-sprayed window of the wheelhouse, I saw that we were within a few hundred yards of that strange area where the tidewaters of Cross Sound met up with the tidewaters of the Pacific Ocean—where the GREEN gives way to the BLUE—the waters between them foaming into a roaring silvery line of froth that stretched as far as the eye could see.

"Just a little chore," Swanson answered, in his most matter-of-fact voice. He appeared busy re-tying a knot on a rope attached to the crosstrees overhead. "It's very simple, really. All you got to do is take that there soaker up to the bow-point, and hop over to the Lacey J with it. Then either Joey or Gabriel, there, will swap you a little something for the fish. You jump back aboard with the something. Simple as that."

Giving the knot a good tug, Swanson slipped past me into the wheelhouse.

Pot. That was the little something Swanson was asking me to risk my neck over. We'd run out of it the day before Pelican and Swanson had just about lost it. When I entered the wheelhouse during a lull, Jimi Hendrix was playing at full volume and Swanson was scratching the bottom of his pipe with a straightened paper clip for resin. Boxes, papers, and magazines were strewn about the wheelhouse; the Pin-Up calendar was torn from the wall; and his coffee cup shattered on the floor. Thankful he hadn't noticed my presence, I'd tiptoed back to my lines and hadn't thought about the episode again until just now.

"You're joking," I said, following Swanson into the wheelhouse. "Really. This is a joke, right?"

Now Swanson was busy grinding the Western World's gears into neutral, then reverse, then forward into low. I had to brace myself by pressing my free hand against the ceiling. Raising the fish to eye level, I continued:

"For a stash of pot you want me to jump boat—"

"Get it out! Get it out!" Swanson started shouting. "Get it out of my face!"

I stood there with a confounded look on my face.

"The fish!" Swanson said. "Get that goddamn fish out of my face! I'm trying to steer the boat, goddamn it!"

Bewildered, I jerked the salmon away from Swanson's face. At that instant, a great groan came up through the floorboards as the Western World lurched into higher gear. That same instant, I toppled headfirst into the dashboard, dropping the salmon onto the floor of the wheelhouse along with pen and pencils and other miscellany from the dash.

Stumbling to my feet again with the salmon, a clipboard, three pencils and a coffee coaster, I apologized for dropping the fish.

"Sorry. I just don't see why we can't—"

"Because I said so!" Swanson interrupted. "This is my boat. If you don't like it . . . pick up your gear and go. Right now. Just pick it up and go. The day I start letting a puller tell me what to do—"

"I ain't telling you what to do!" I interrupted, raising my voice at Swanson for the first time. "Just let me know why we can't throw the bloody fish across instead of me risking my neck jumping!"

Both of us were surprised by my sudden outburst. There was an awkward silence for several seconds as we looked at and away from each other at the same time. Finally, Swanson spoke:

"We ain't throwing it across, goddamn it, because it's too damn easy to lose that way."

The Lacey J was pulling up alongside our prow again. Through the wheelhouse window, I saw the man on deck had moved up to the Lacey J's bow-point. He was crouched there on a knee, pointing at his wristwatch.

"All right," I heard myself saying.

Without another word between us, I took my rain slicker down from its nail on the wall and left the wheelhouse, thinking, the man is relentless.

Walking up that bow-point was about as easy as walking up the curve of a banana. The gales went unchecked here: strong enough to knock over a small child; and, quite possibly, a full grown man trying to balance a hangover, a twenty-pound fish, and a dozen other thoughts completely unrelated to the task he was performing—the most recurrent of these being that if he had any sense at all he'd up and quit on the spot; have Swanson deliver his own goddamn fish; fetch his own pot; etc., etc.

"How goes it?" came a voice over the wind and blasts of water against the Western World's flank.

It was the fisherman crouched on the bow of the Lacey J; the one Swanson had referred to as Gabriel. He had a large red face that matched his stocking cap. I guessed it was a face made red as much from drink as from the elements: a sad but generous face. Overtop of a long-sleeved thermal shirt, Gabriel wore a black T-shirt with some faded lettering across the chest.

ANYONE CAN BE A FATHER. . .
BUT IT TAKES SOMEONE SPECIAL
TO BE A DADDY!

I wondered if Gabriel's wife had gotten him the shirt before or after she'd started fooling around on him.

I was past the anchor windlass now. From here out, I was on my own. There were no ropes or cables to hold onto now, no wheelhouse to fall back on: just the sky above, the sea below, and this terrible oblivion tottering all around me.

"Great!" I called back, fearing another spoken work might send me over.

"Just go easy!" Gabriel encouraged. "This is nuts—but, if you take your time, it'll be all right!"

I found myself glancing out at the water too much. It was fine when my sights were set on the course of the water, but when I redirected my sights to the course I was taking along the bow I discovered that the very boards I stood on tended to run out beneath me also.

"Hey, kid! Slow it down. And keep low!"

Gabriel again. I glanced up long enough to see that he was acting out what he meant by "keep low": squatting up and down like an overgrown baboon.

"Got it! Keep low," I heard myself repeating. "Keep low." I reprimanded myself for thinking Gabriel looked comical. This advice just might save my life.

Aping Gabriel, I inched my way along that mile-long last five feet to the end of the bow-point. . .thinking, and, at the same time, trying not think, about those war horror stories regarding soldiers who crap their pants in the line of fire. I'd always laughed right along with my schoolmates at the thought. I wasn't laughing now.

"Holy Christ. . ." I whispered, when I'd made it to that edge.

I took a knee and waved at Gabriel.

"What the hell are we doing here?" I braved across the wave and foam.

But Gabriel didn't seem to hear me even though we were only fifteen feet away: fifteen feet, that is, at a given moment. It all depended on the rise and fall our two bows. Our trawlers were rising and falling on the beginning of open ocean troughs. At one moment, you'd become elevated on a mound of water; then, the next, this mound would cave in and you'd find yourself at the bottom of a watery bowl, with nothing to see around you but climbing walls of water.

"Stay down!"

Gabriel was instructing me to remain crouched while Swanson edged our prow closer to the Lacey J. Soon, our bows were seesawing about ten feet apart. Gabriel stood up and moved to the edge of his trawler's bow. He signaled me to remain crouched while the trawler's inched closer.

It wouldn't be long now. My breathing quickened to match my heart. My mouth and throat were dry and I wished I drank more water after vomiting in the hull. Our bows were rising and falling opposite each other now. When one came up, the other came down. It made me shudder to think what would happen if I should somehow wound up in that no-man's land of water between the two heaving bows. For a second, I imagined my body floating face down in dead man fashion between the boats . . . my green rain slicker puffed up with air. Then, the next second, one of the two hulls would come smashing down on top of me—busting my skull open like a watermelon; my body repeatedly throttled by the hulls of the two trawlers until I was, inadvertently, pushed aside. Then Swanson, or the men aboard the Lacey J, dragging my carcass out of the spume with a long-handled gaff.

"Hey! Heads up! If you're gonna jump—now's the time!"

Shakily, I stood up, holding onto the anchor until I was sure of my balance.

"You all right?" Gabriel asked. He was within eight feet of me now. "Want to call this damn thing off?"

"No," I said, forcing a smile. "I got it."

The boats were dangerously close now. Not only did I fear making the jump, but now had the additional worry that our two prows might collide.

I toed my way to very edge of the bow. I switched the salmon into my other hand to assure a better grip. Then, carefully timing my jump midway between the rise and fall of our two bows, I leaped across to the Lacey J.

Gabriel was there to greet me as I landed on the bow of the Lacey J. In my zeal to make it across, I'd jumped a little too far. If Gabriel hadn't been there to catch me, I might have continued right on over the other side of the Lacey J.

"Guess I overdid it a little," I joked.

"I'd say!" said Gabriel. "Had me thinking you were Michael Jordan a second there!"

We laughed at the slapstick notion of me going into the drink on the other side.

A couple of seagulls were circling overhead. Pointing toward the gulls, I said:

"Maybe they were waiting for me?"

"Yeah!" Gabriel laughed. "Right!"

A fresh gale blew across the bow the Lacey J. Both of us were relieved when it let up.

I turned the nearly thawed salmon over to Gabriel.

He handed me an ounce of weed in a Ziploc sandwich bag, and, in a second sandwich bag, a fistful of twenty-dollar bills.

"What's this for?" I asked.

Gabriel's face flushed.

"You'll have to ask your skipper about that?"

Apparently, the stash of pot was not the only reason Swanson had sent me here.

Gabriel turned—as though to leave—then turned back—offering me his hand.

"What's your name, kid?"

"Adam," I said.

"Adam, huh?" Gabriel said, scratching the back of one of his big red ears. "Well . . . good luck, Adam. You're doing something I could never do."

Gabriel glanced uneasily towards Swanson.

"Worked a whole summer with that son of a bitch ten years ago. Wouldn't do it again for all the tea in China."

Then, raising the salmon as though to give reason for his hurry, Gabriel walked back to the Lacey J's wheelhouse.

I looked towards Joey at the wheel. Joey was pointing emphatically past me towards the bow-point. The reason for his urgency was apparent at a glance: our trawlers were pulling apart. Already there was a good eight feet of space between them.

Shoving the two stashes in the front pockets of my jeans, I hurried to the edge of the Lacey J. I leapt back aboard our boat while the Western World's bow was still coming up. I landed somewhat successfully—falling hard on my knees beside the anchor.

I returned Swanson's thumbs up from the wheel, then remained crouched on the bow as our two trawlers pulled apart. I saw Gabriel emerge on deck again for an instant, then disappear inside the Lacey J's wheelhouse.

Who was this Gabriel?

What else could he tell me about Swanson?

Or—better stated—what could he tell me about him that I did not already know?

When the other fisherman on the Lacey J, Joey, waved goodbye from the wheel . . . I did not wave back.

Chapter Twelve

China Harry's Fish Buyer

It was near midnight before Swanson announced we were done fishing that first day on the Esther Island grounds.

The day had been a success: the biggest single-day catch we'd had yet. The annual Esther Island King Salmon Run had occurred on the day predicted. Our ice holds had become so filled that the last dozen salmon had to be left in the cooler above deck until we arrived at tonight's fish-buyer. Yet, as I staggered out of my four by three by two foot sunken box at the rear of the Western World, I could not help feel indifferent towards it all. Though I'd caught, cleaned and packed each one of these fish with my own hands, there had been something lacking in the way I'd gone about doing this.

The afternoon run had gone smooth enough. After the chaotic episodes of that morning, the numbing routine of the drag had been something of a comfort. The act of bashing salmon brains had been a kind of release. I'd been knocking them cold with one blow most the day, as opposed to the several clubbings it usually took. But, by late afternoon, even landing and killing the catch had lost its thrill. By that point, the numbers of fish had begun to take their toll. Like too much of a good thing, the salmon kept coming in without let-up. One after another . . . until catching them became as engaging as drawing laundry from a clothesline. Instead of anticipating the possibility of a star forty-pounder on the end of a tag-line, I found myself dreading the probability there was one.

We were entering a small sheltered bay a few miles north of Esther Island. After spending most the day on a pitching, rolling ocean, it was a comfort to see cliffs and mountains— actual land!—rising on three sides of us. The sun had ducked behind the frozen peaks of Mt. Saint Elias only moments ago. There was still enough light out that I could see a gang of sea otters perched atop a large floating log towards shore. The otters had stopped their clowning to watch us drift by.

Swanson called me to the wheel.

"How's the hand?" Swanson asked.

I took my post at the wheel.

"Stiff," I said, showing how difficult it was to make a fist with my left hand. "It keeps getting stiffer. Like I got arthritis in it."

I remembered the surprise and shock I'd felt just a few hours ago when I'd unknowingly grabbed a Ling Cod around the gills while removing a troublesome hook. The moment I'd performed this blunder poison had been injected into my palm from the spines hidden beneath the Ling Cod's gills. I could still feel the sting from the red spot in the middle of my palm where the spines had first pricked me.

"Arthritis, huh?" Swanson grinned. "Ah, well!" He slapped me on the back. "Stiffness don't last long anyway. Should be out come tomorrow morning. Best thing you can do now is keep it moving. Work it out."

I thought Swanson had winked at me, but couldn't be sure.

On the backside of this bay was a long flat-bottomed fish-buying scow we were to sell today's catch. I could read HARRY'S FISH-BUYER on a large red and white hand-painted sign on the scow's rooftop. Another trawler was pulled alongside the fish-buyer, preparing to leave. The deckhand on this vessel had just untied his trawler and was recoiling the stay line on his back deck. He was exchanging goodbyes with a little man smoking a pipe on the scow's front porch. I figured this man was the proprietor because of the excessive manner in which he nodded his head in agreement with what the other fellow was saying. How many times had I seen my own father back home in Couer d' Alene nod to customers at the hardware store in just such a manner!

"Heads up!" Swanson shouted—so I jerked the wheel way over the right in my astonishment. "Come on. Straighten her out. Let her down a gear. See if we can't coast in from here out. . ."

Eventually, I got us back on course. I was slaphappy at the wheel: smiling—even laughing—at the curt remarks Swanson made towards me. I shook my head to get some of the tiredness out. I felt oddly detached from what I was doing at the wheel. It was as though I was translucent: my mind and body so worn out from work and lack of rest that the steering wheel felt like a toy under my work-numbed hands. Maybe coffee would help? But I'd already drunk so much I was beginning to wonder if hadn't replaced the blood in my veins.

And like the butt of a mercilessly repeated bad joke, Swanson was right on cue offering more NO-DOZE tablets:

"Ah, come on," Swanson said. "It'll give you a little pick-up."

Swanson dry-gulped two of the tablets himself.

"Ah, yes!" he continued. "That's the ticket! Go ahead. You'll be thanking me by the time we're through unloading that shit load out back."

Unload! I thought. Somehow, I'd imagined there'd be a crew to unload the catch for us like there had been in Pelican.

"Yeah. . ." Swanson said, winking this time for sure. "Just you and me and that big catch. . ."

I took the caffeine tablets.

The proprietor was through with his goodbyes to the other fisherman now. He ducked through the large sliding door of the fish-buyer, then re-emerged wearing a yellow rain jacket and stuffing a fresh pinch of tobacco into his long wooden pipe. He smiled and waved us forward, then commenced to lighting his pipe by running a match up the zipper of his rain jacket.

"All right," I heard Swanson call from somewhere on deck. "Put her back in gear and creep up with her real soft. When she gets alongside the scow slide her in reverse. I'll jump boat and signal from the scow when to cut her off. She's all mine after that."

China Harry.

We were unloading the catch Chinese Fire Drill style: I down in the holds tossing the ice-caked salmon up to Swanson on deck. . .who in turn tossed it to China Harry onboard the scow. . .who stacked them neatly in a roll-away cart.

I'd forgotten the nickname Swanson had ascribed to the fish-buyer until Swanson referred to him as such while introducing us.

"This here's China Harry," Swanson said.

"How do you do, Adam?" said China Harry.

"Fine. Thanks," I answered.

I'd been briefed about China Harry.

"We call him China Harry," Swanson had explained. "'Cuz he looks and acts like one of them Chinamen you see on TV and at the movies. You know the type. Always smiling and bobbing, bobbing and smiling. Yes, sir. No, sir. Never talks back. Lucky if you get two words out of him. That sorta thing."

"Truth is," Swanson had confessed. "China Harry ain't anymore Chinese than you or I. He's Tlingit—like Miss Sue Ann Bonnet. Rumor has it he's just as much a sucker for all that hocus-pocus horseshit as Sue Ann! Lotta guys think he's an old American Indian Movement activist from the 60's. They boycott his buyer 'cuz of it. . ."

". . . but not me. I don't judge a man by the color of the flag he flies. Besides, if you really want to hear it, China Harry's just an old flake. A fag. 'Course now that's my opinion. Thing is when it gets right down to it China Harry's as good a man as any other. Never cheats a fisherman at the scales. Doesn't give us a lot of lip like a lotta these new fish-buyers from the lower-48 do. Always gives top dollar for a clean catch. And that's saying something out here, boy! Believe me, that's saying something."

China Harry was all and more than Swanson had forewarned. He was a strangely effeminate little man. His features were plainly Indian: the high, rather delicate cheekbones, the blunt nose, broad mouth and fleshy skin. And his expressions, gestures, facial posturing were, indeed, of the Chinese stereotype he was trying to emulate. If China Harry was a sign he would have read EXCUSE ME MAY I HELP YOU. He was the last type of man I expected to encounter in so remote a part of the planet as this.

Yet, in a funny way Swanson had failed to mention, there was also something similar about China Harry's appearance to that of Philip Swanson's. Both were small, ageless looking men; both had the same beady set of eyes; and, most essentially, both had that puppet-like grotesqueness about their character:

Swanson because of his crippled shoulder, China Harry because of his absurd efforts to appear an absurd Chinese stereotype. They were flipsides of the same coin: Swanson the grotesque of the hard masculine man and China Harry that of the soft feminine one. Yet this softness of China Harry's was deceiving. I learned this after shaking hands with the man and then, a few minutes later, observing how these same spongy soft hands had proved so apt at handling the catch.

Tossing the last King salmon up to Swanson, I climbed out of the holds, and helped him and China Harry wheel the rollaway inside the fish-buyer.

The chrome-plated scales were set in the middle of the large rectangular room. There were three actual scales. They reminded me of the ones in the produce section of the IGA store in Couer d' Alene that my mother had scolded me and my brothers and sisters for pulling on when we were children.

"China Harry," Swanson said, as the first three salmon were laid on the scales. "You sure you haven't rigged this scale? This one on the right looks a little off center to me." Swanson nudged me with an elbow. "You wouldn't be trying to pull a fast one on a couple of dumb, tired fishermen, would 'ya?"

China Harry smiled slyly back, his tobacco-stained teeth clenched down on the stem of his pipe. He took his eyes away from the scales only to punch numbers on his adding machine. He said nothing.

"That's what I thought!" Swanson joked, nudging me again.

While Swanson and China Harry discussed the current market price for King and Coho salmon, I wandered to a far corner of the room where two large shelves of books reached towards the ceiling. Beside the books was a padded rocking chair . . . beside the chair, a thermos of coffee and clean coffee mugs.

There was a hand-written sign on the wall that read: THESE BOOKS ARE NOT FOR SALE . . . BUT FEEL FREE TO BROWSE IF YOU MUST. I smiled at China Harry's use of the phrase IF YOU MUST.

There was a smattering of Louis L'Armour and Zane Grey westerns, some Tom Clancy and Ken Follet spy thrillers, but most of the books were of scholarly-type. I'd read or heard of some of the titles: RICHARD II by Shakespeare . . . ORIGIN OF THE SPECIES and THE DESCENT OF MAN by Darwin. But then there were others I hadn't heard of: THE GOLDEN BOUGH by Sir James Frazier. . .DECLINE OF THE WEST by Oswald Spengler. . .ONE HUNDRED YEARS OF SOLITUDE. . .WAITING FOR GODOT. . .THE TIBETAN BOOK OF THE DEAD. There were two full rows of Indian histories: NOW THAT THE BUFFALO'S GONE . . . BLACK ELK SPEAKS . . . BURY MY HEART AT WOUNDED KNEE. Half the names of the funny foreign authors I couldn't even pronounce: like THE TECHNOLOGICAL SOCIETY and PROPAGANDA: THE FORMATION OF MEN'S ATTITUDES by Jacques Ellul. I laughed at the way my tongue kept tripping over the last name of this author.

"Do you like books?" China Harry asked.

"Yes," I said, glancing back at the shelves. "The little that I've read."

Actually, I love books and had declared English as my major at U of Idaho that coming fall. But I was feeling a bit intimidated by the selections I saw on China Harry's shelves.

"Have you read all these yourself?" I asked.

"Ninety-nine percent of them," China Harry said, laying three new salmon on the scales. "It gets very lonely here. It's nice to be able to read about faraway places and other peoples and other worlds. Don't you think so?"

"No frigate like a book!" I said.

"Oh! Very good!" China Harry said. "Emily Dickinson. . ."

Then I said something that made China Harry stop smiling—for a moment. Swanson had returned to the Western World for some reason, and I took advantage of the opportunity.

"Harry," I said. "If the fishing's really as bad as some people say it's getting . . . how come we keep catching so many fish?"

I was fully aware of the bluntness of my question. But Swanson might return at any moment.

China Harry hesitated, puffing on his pipe several times. Then, in one word, he answered:

"Canada."

My mind flashbacked to the conversation between the three fishermen in line behind me at the Elfin Grocer. I remembered something about tolls and Mounties and dams on the Columbia River and no dams on the Fraser River.

"You're kidding!" I said. "These are Fraser River salmon?"

China Harry nodded.

"Son of a bitch!" I said. I felt like someone who has been searching for something only to find it right beneath his or her nose. "That's how we keep our numbers high—and beat the regulators! By intercepting Canadian salmon—"

"And the Canadians do the same!" China Harry replied. "Both sides are fighting over what's left in the barrel. When this resource is exhausted, we'll be fighting over another as yet unnamed one! It's the human condition. It's how we are as a species."

I was overwhelmed. All this . . . and China Harry with his same poker face . . . was marking another fish's weight down on his note pad.

"But Harry. . ." I said. "How can you know all this and still be part of it?"

I realized the brashness of my question—not to mention its hypocritical nature—after the fact. When I began to apologize, China Harry smiled and said:

"Remember, Adam . . . there are always three shells in a shell game."

Just then Swanson came clomping back on the scow, fooling with his fly. When he saw me standing gape-mouthed by the books, he motioned me over.

"What's going on here?" Swanson joked. "I expect you to keep an eye on the Chinaman while I'm away. No telling what China Harry's capable of!"

We were towards the end of the catch now. There was a little chute behind the scales leading down to the holds beneath the floor. China Harry grabbed the three salmon he'd just weighed under the gills and sent them headfirst down the chute. I wondered if Swanson had eavesdropped on our conversation. I was more confused now than ever. What had China Harry meant by three shells in a shell game? Was he implying that the First Nations could regain control of their old salmon grounds after the U.S. and Canada were busy duking it out over what was left of the salmon pie? And what if the First Nations could pull off this shell game? What would they alone be able to do to save the salmon?

The room was strangely quiet. There was only the familiar pattern of the scale's squeaking as new salmon were laid on them, then the sound of digits being punched out on the adding machine, then the salmon being shot down the chute to the holds below. Outside, the wind had stopped blowing and it was eerily still. There was only the tinkle of bilge water being pumped out of the Western World's bulwarks.

To break the monotony—and cover-up the sentiments of my conversation with China Harry (in case Swanson HAD been eavesdropping)—I cleared my throat and joked:

"Guess we pulled in quite a haul today—hey, Phil?"

"Yeah. . ."Swanson said, after a pause. "I suppose you could say that."

China Harry was having difficulty laying a larger-sized King on the scale properly. Swanson had to reach over and hold the salmon by the tail while China Harry took the reading.

"Oh, yeah," I continued—since Swanson had nothing else to say. "I've been meaning to ask what kind of percentage of the catch I'm getting. I would have brought it up sooner—"

"Hmm—" I heard Swanson grunt.

Swanson seemed irritated about something. I wasn't sure if it was something I'd said or if it was the seeming trouble he and China Harry were having with another large salmon.

"Excuse me," I said. "I suppose we can talk about this later—"

"No-no," Swanson interrupted, free to address me now that this salmon had been weighed. "Now's as good a time as any. Funny we haven't gotten round to it sooner. Hmm, now? Let's see. . ."

I reached over and held the tail of a large Coho while Swanson mulled over figures both aloud and in his head.

"Yes. . ." China Harry said, almost to himself. "You are new out here."

"How can you tell?" I said, trying to be a good sport.

Smiling pleasantly, China Harry continued:

"Well, among other things, by the way this catch has been cleaned."

"What?" I said, feeling betrayed.

China Harry opened the slit belly of the salmon in his hands and ran one of his fingers along a section of meat I had cut against the grain on. "But," he finished, "not damaged so much as to devalue THIS fish."

I smiled back weakly.

China Harry was definitely a player.

"Harry?" Swanson asked. "What's the going price on Co-ho's this week?"

"Three twenty-five a pound, Philip."

"And Kings?"

"Four-ten."

"Thanks," said Swanson.

At last, Swanson turned to me and concluded:

"Ten percent of the catch is the going rate. Including today—and those three good days we had before Pelican—I figure we've grossed somewhere in the neighborhood of three-thousand by this point. Ten percent of three thousand is three hundred. Roughly, three hundred dollars."

"Three hundred dollars?" I repeated. I wondered if Swanson meant three-hundred for today and those three good days before Pelican exclusively.

"Is that three hundred for the entire season?"

"Yeah," Swanson said. "Unless," he continued, smiling to-wards China Harry. "Unless the Chinaman wants to give us a bonus for bringing in such a pretty catch! What ya' say, Harry? Handing out any bonuses today?"

China Harry smiled and shook his head.

Swanson laughed out loud.

"Three hundred dollars?" I repeated again. I began to figure out how much that came out to per hour after all I'd worked these last two and a half weeks.

"Of course," Swanson added, as though an afterthought. "I'll have knock off for expenses and such . . . you understand."

I stopped figuring and looked at Swanson. It crossed my mind he might be joking. I tried smiling at him. He did not smile back.

"Yeah. Expenses. . ." Swanson said. With a grunt, he explained: "Do I look like the Governor of Alaska to you?"

When I didn't reply, just continued to stare back in disbelief, Swanson continued:

"Well, now. I'll have to knock off at least fifty food, another fifty for gear lost . . . little things. . like that brand new scrub brush you knocked overhead on opening day. And then there was your fun at the Elbow Room and your little fling at Roxie's. . ." He winked devilishly at me. "Heck!" Swanson concluded, grinning again. "I guess that breaks us about even, don't it?"

I felt dizzy. I couldn't believe I was hearing this. Even! After all the work! These long days! No sleep! It occurred to me that Swanson might even be screwing me over on the three-thousand dollar gross. Intuitively, I knew the figure was more in the four thousand range. But there was no way I could prove this. I'd been so busy orienting myself to my new job and new surroundings that it had never occurred to me to keep any kind of record. I'd never signed any kind of contract to work for Philip Swanson—never filled out a W-2 or passed along my social security number. I was entirely beholden to Swanson's judgment. This seemed too terribly stupid to actually be happening!

I turned towards China Harry, but his mask was firmly in place. He'd finished weighing the last of the catch and was tapping out the bottom of his pipe. His wet red lips were puckered in a frown. But I couldn't tell if it was because of what he'd just witnessed or because of the trouble he was having cleaning the bowl of his pipe.

"Even?" I said. "How could that be?"

There was a Styrofoam ice chest filled with packages of frozen herring at our feet. Swanson was turning over one of these cellophane wrapped packages in his hands now.

"Harry?" Swanson said, ignoring me. "These just come in today?"

China Harry had cleared his pipe and was repacking the bowl with more of his cherry-flavored tobacco.

"Yes," China Harry said, lighting his pipe. "Just this morning, Philip. From Seattle."

"Seattle, huh?" Swanson said. "All right, then. I'll talk six of these Puget Sound puppies."

China Harry punched out the cost of each herring packet individually.

"Excuse me," I said, stepping closer to Swanson. "Excuse me. I don't understand. I don't get it."

"Goddamn it," Swanson mumbled. China Harry had handed him a clipboard with a bill of sale on it. Swanson scribbled out his signature on the bottom line. Then he tore out the carbon copy receipt of sale, folded it, and stuffed it in a breast pocket of his shirt.

"Goddamn," he repeated. "I just told you why! Expenses!"

"Yeah. . ." I said. "O.K. But after all the hours I've worked—"

"Hours?" Swanson interrupted. "Hours, boy? You are a green one, aren't you? Come on—get with it—man! Everything's based on percentages out here . . . like I been telling you since the start. Percentages. That's why we work these long crazy hours. I'm hoping things will pick up from here out. If we can fill the holds in four hour's time tomorrow—fine! We'll call it a day! But if it takes until midnight, then we'll be working till midnight. That's just the way things work out here. Got to give up those old wage-slave ideas!"

"And put my trust in you?"

"That's right," said Swanson, unable to hold back a little smirk. "Put your trust in me."

Swanson paused to slide a pinch of chewing tobacco under his upper lip. He offered me a pinch. When I declined, he shook his head slowly and placed the lid in a rear pocket of his jeans. After a long pause, he finished:

"Now I wasn't going to tell you this until the season ended . . . but . . . if things continue to work out . . . and you stay on for sockeye season . . . well, I'll be upping your percentage to 15%. By that time, I figure you'll be worth the extra 5% to me."

Before I could respond, Swanson shuffled past me towards one of the open doors.

Turning around, I saw that China Harry was already out of the porch in front of Swanson. Both were waving hello as a new trawler, heavy with fish, came alongside the scow.

Chapter Thirteen

Little Red Meat

Near the end of the next day on Esther Island, I began releasing salmon from our lines. . .

I was bringing in the tag-lines when the idea occurred to me. The rain had slowed to a drizzle. Instead of having to wipe my face every five seconds to see what I was doing, I had to only do this every minute or so. Already two of the tag-lines were in. The first had come back with its bait still on, the second with its bait missing. Unfortunately, this third and present tag line was proving more difficult. The small King salmon on the end of it was determined not to be brought in in an orderly manner. Three times it had jumped out of the water trying to spit its hook. It had nose-dived so sharply a moment ago that I'd lost the line part of the tag and had had to re-thread and re-coil the line through my fingertips all over again. This was particularly maddening now that I was so close to finishing. I was sweating beneath my raingear and was looking forward to stripping myself of it in the dry of wheelhouse. Finally, the fish seemed to be relenting: sixty-feet off starboard side, rolling side to side in our wake.

I'd been brooding all day over what I'd learned at HAR-RY'S FISH-BUYER. Having discovered that I'd earned no money, my work seemed pointless. Remembering Old Judge Peterson's remark that in the "old days" a green hand worked without pay just to learn the ropes, I realized I'd been wrong in expecting so much so fast with my modern day sensibilities. But was it wrong to expect something for my misery? Add to the equation that we were probably pirating Canada bound salmon on these Esther Island grounds and my work seemed worse than pointless: I, Adam Porter, was a shanghaied slave in Captain Swanson's galley!

Humiliating stuff . . .

The salmon was along the left side of the trawler now, on about fifteen feet of line. I could see where the hook was set in a corner of its mouth. A few more feet and I'd be able to gaff and land it. The dry of the wheelhouse seemed that much closer. I could almost feel it beneath my damp clothing. And what was that skunky smell coming through the open door of the wheelhouse? Wasn't it my turn to pack and smoke a big bowl of my own?

I stepped out of the cockpit with my right foot, bracing it against the trawler's fender. I grabbed one of the three gaffs hanging by their hooks along the rim of the cockpit. Apparently, the fish was played out, on its side now. Threading the fish in, I began to talk out loud to it. This talk had become an occasional habit of mine to make the long hours pass.

"Well, hell, Little Red Meat," I began, switching my gaff carefully from my left to right hand. "What's the sense of looking at me like that? You suppose I wanted all this trouble? Hell, if it was up to me, I'd have cut you loose long ago!"

With a start, I noticed that Little Red Meat wasn't quite as played out as I'd imagined. Three strong swipes of his tail assured me of that.

He was as close as I was going to get him. All that remained was walking him a little more to my left, then gaffing him just beneath the gills. But this had to be done very carefully and very quickly. The wood beneath my boots was extremely slick because of the drizzle. Also, there was always the chance a large swell might sneak up on me even though we were moving inland now.

"Come on, Red Meat. Take it easy," I bantered, having to lean a little more over the side than I'd care to. "What's all the fuss? This thing's got nothing to do between me and you. It ain't up to us. I get paid for bringing you in because there's these things call People in places like Seattle and New York and San Francisco who pay big bucks to squeeze you between crackers! It sucks. But all of us—and that goes for you too, my friend—are subject to the demands of the market economy. Crazy, huh?"

I stopped talking. For an instant, the sun broke through the clouds, and I saw my shadow on the water, reaper-like with my hood and gaff in hand. Then, an instant later, my shadow dissolved as the clouds closed around the sun again.

Dizzied, I stepped back up on the fender. The rapid, needle-like rains made the water around me sizzle, adding to the surrealness of the scene. Time to quit screwing around. If I didn't get out of this cockpit soon, I'd wind up going overboard, for sure. Vision or no visions.

"All right, little bastard! That's it. Either you're coming aboard or I'm going in after you. Let's go!"

Little Red Meat was in position now. All I had to do was hitch him out of the water a foot or two, and plant the gaff-hook. Easy enough. But when I tried to lift him clear of the water, he did the very thing I'd feared all along. He rolled in against the fender.

"Sneaky little bastard!"

I chucked my gaff to the bottom of the cockpit. If I hadn't been fooling around talking with a goddamn fish I'd be inside packing that bowl right now. Was I losing my mind? Unable to actually see Little Red Meat, I could hear and feel him flailing against the husk of the fender.

This was a bad situation all the way around. If I tried to raise him from the water, from where I stood, the hook would strip. I could climb out of the cockpit, walk him alongside the trawler's flank and land him at mid-deck. But by that time, the meat might be damaged to the point we couldn't even sell it.

There was, of course, one other option.

I checked over my shoulder to see that Swanson wasn't on deck. Sometimes he came out to check on our progress. But the deck proved clear. A flap of steadying sail had come undone again; a loose Styrofoam cup was alternately being swept across deck and then smashed up against the outer wall of the wheelhouse. It was the same empty stage I'd been looking at all day.

Turning around, I gave the line a sharp little tug. Little Red Meat spit the hook, shooting out backwards in our wake, away from the trawler.

"Adios, amigos!" I joked, thrilled at the sight of and the feel of the limp tag-line flapping in the breeze. "Tell the others not to come!"

Although I know it is scientifically impossible, Little Red Mean winked at me.

He really did.

Releasing Little Red Meat felt so good, that I immediately released his two sisters—Medium-Sized Red Meat and Great Big Red Meat—on the last two tag-lines. Stumbling back into the cockpit when I'd finished, I laughed out loud. Why hadn't

I thought of this before? A wonderful healthy antidote to my despair! For every dollar Swanson swindled from me—I'd release salmon in kind. Set our balance straight—with interest added, of course.

I returned to my work refreshed; my faith in justice restored; my sentiments of goodwill towards our Canadian neighbors sated. I took extra pains coiling up these last three tag-lines, laying them neatly beside their somewhat tangled mates.

Like an omen from above, the rain and drizzle stopped. For the first time since noon, I was able to remove my raingear and let my body breathe. Through a large saucer-like opening in the clouds, the yellow Alaskan sun brought everything brilliantly back to life. The green green of the tree-rich islands and blue blue of the sparkling sea! 18,000 foot Mt. Saint Elias's snow-capped peaks glowed bright orange and pink and white on the horizon, apparition-like, a distant Shangri-La! From now on, I'd keep tabs on how many fish we caught. And there'd be no more running around in dives like Roxie's Kitchen. No, sir! From here out I'd walk the straight and narrow. Besides, even if the wages were low and the grub was worse, where else in the U.S. of A could one work and live and breathe in such magnificent surroundings!

Turning to climb out of the cockpit, I saw Philip Swanson moving about on deck.

"Here we go. . ." I whispered aloud, my heart pumping loud.

Swanson was hanging the four tires we used as bumper when mooring. He'd been hoisting one of them over the side the moment I'd spotted him. I would openly confront him about the salmon I'd released. Obviously, he was letting on that he hadn't seen me release them. But he must have! He was probably just waiting for the right time to nail me with it. But I'd tell him before he told me: and let him know what he could do about it.

Beat the bastard to the punch. . .

He was standing directly above me now, behind the hayrack. He'd finished laying out the tires, and was smoking pot from his pipe. Through the cables and fairlead blocks, I could see he was surveying the waters behind us. His predatory eyes roved from one side of the open inlet to the other; not focusing on anything in particular. I thought of the improbability that someone, even someone with as good an eye as Swanson's, could spot any of the salmon if they'd bellied up after I'd released them. By our present pace, the last salmon released was no closer than 200 yards in our wake, and the first salmon, Little Red Meat, a quarter mile behind.

"Look!" Swanson said, his eyes fixing on something directly behind us. "Behind you!"

"What?" I shouted, shading my eyes from the glare coming off the water. "I don't see a thing."

"No!" came Swanson's reply. He'd moved closer, standing with one foot along the rim of the cockpit. He pointed towards the sky with the stem of his brass pipe. "Up there. Coming out from the trees."

There, appearing out of the shadows along shore, a huge bald eagle flew in a direct path towards where Little Red Meat would be if still floundering on the surface. The eagle's great wings flapped slow and steady through the air. When it reached the area, about a quarter mile in our wake, it began to circle. Then suddenly, as though one of its wings had broken in midflight, the eagle dropped from the sky. It spiraled down towards the glittering water, righting itself at the last moment with a furious pumping of wings. The large, hand-like talons broke the sea's surface, emerging a second later with Little Red Meat. Its wings still pumping, the great bird lifted itself and the salmon from the water, Little Red Meat's tail wagging in protest. In the same slow deliberate manner it had arrived, the eagle departed: flying the other way down the long stretch of inlet.

I was dumbfounded. All this had happened within a matter of minutes.

"Is that something else or what!" Swanson said. He stepped back from the cockpit: a horrible-smile and glazed-over look to his eye. "Damn! Look at that bird go!"

"You know. . ." Swanson continued. "It's funny . . . but I can always see this sort of thing happening way ahead of time. Even before the bird starts circling . . . something to do with the way its wings are flapping. It just ain't flapping about like it sometimes does, but flying with that true purpose. Know what I mean?"

I smiled to show that I did.

Then Swanson said something to completely throw me:

"Well . . . keep up the good work."

Mumbling something about expecting a call over the wire, Swanson reminded me to swab both the cockpit and main deck before coming in. Finally, without another word, without the slightest sign or gesture that he'd known a thing about any of the salmon I'd released, he returned to the wheelhouse.

My face burning in humiliation, I returned to my chores. Filling the bucket with water, I began to swab deck, scrubbing so hard that the steel fiber on my brush broke off against the wood.

It was no good.

I couldn't beat him.

Even old Mother Nature was on his side!

These days were getting too long. Much much too long . . .

Chapter Fourteen

The Beast Below

When I entered the wheelhouse fifteen minutes later, I discovered my day had gotten even longer.

"Howdy-howdy-howdy!" Swanson said, swiveling around in his stool. "Got things wrapped up back there?"

I nodded, hanging my raingear on its nail by the door and shouldering the sliding door shut to minimize the drafts.

I had not failed to notice that Swanson was smiling: always a bad sign.

I reveled in the light and warmth of the wheelhouse. Steam was already lifting off my raingear, blood beginning to circulate through my freezing hands and face again. CCR was playing on the stereo, but not so loud as to be annoying. Best of all, Swanson had brewed a pot of coffee. I would have a cup before retiring to the hull to string gear for tomorrow morning's run. Then maybe smoke a little weed, and off to never-never land.

A fragmented message cracked over the CB radio: something or other about "when would be a good time" and "if you want we could—": the far off, somehow familiar voices coming through no better than that.

"What's up?" I asked.

Swanson switched the radio off and turned the stereo back on low volume.

"Got some good news. Remember the Rapp brothers from Pelican?"

I nodded.

How could I forget.

"Well. . ." Swanson said, eyes twinkling. "I just got word they're passing through Esther Island on way to Elfin Cove. Being in the area and all. . .I did the neighborly thing and invited them and a few other boys over for a late night game of cards. From the sound of their last call, I'd say they're somewhere up around Cape Spencer about now. Ought to be here by the time we finish with our business at HARRY'S . . ."

HARRY'S! I thought. The holds! We'd filled them with salmon a second day in a row. In my sleepwalking-like state, I'd completely overlooked the fact we would have to unload this catch before we filled up with another. And now this late night card party too?

"What about sleep?" I said.

Swanson slapped my back, spilling more coffee on my shirtfront.

"Don't worry about that," he said, winking at me now. "This bit about the card party's only the half of it."

"What's the other half?"

"The real news," Swanson said, "is the big snowstorm Tom and Hank ran into on the way up from Sitka."

"Snowstorm?" I said, looking out at the clear evening. "What are you talking about—"

"Not that kind of snow!" Swanson interrupted.

He placed the back of his thumb to his nose and made a snorting gesture.

"Oh," I said. "That kind of snow."

HARRY'S FISH-BUYER came into view now; several figures knotted together on the scow's front porch.

"Woo-wee!" Swanson said, cranking the volume on the stereo. "Only the dead sleep tonight, boys!"

"Yeah . . . hit me."

"Me, too."

"Nope, I'm staying."

"Yep. . ."

"Yep. . ."

"Well, all right. But next time I cut the deck!"

Laughter.

"O.K! O.K! Place your bets, girlies. Or drop out while you still got the chance!"

More laughter.

The hull was packed. Besides Tom and Hank Rapp, four fishermen I'd never met had come aboard. We sat crunched up around a flat board that had been wrestled down from upstairs, on turned over crates and buckets so our knees stuck out over the low-lying table. All of us had had our share of the 100-proof refined powder of the coca plant—and all of us, including yours truly, had been reduced to a Neanderthal state by it.

I'd played the first dozen hands, but when I lost on a full house of three kings and two queens to Philip Swanson's Royal Flush . . . I rejected his repeat offer of another $20 loan to get me back in the game. By his accounting, it would take another week to settle the account on my original $20 ante as it was.

I sat just outside the circle now: a handkerchief to my runny nose, thinking maybe, just maybe, I'd sneak in a few winks between now and first light.

"All right! Settle down, you turkeys!" the dealer called out. "Settle down! Bets are on the table. Now show your cards, or forever hold your cod-piece, amen!"

The players laid down their cards. When Tom Rapp won—a third consecutive time—they went wild:

"What's this? Tom Rapp? Again? How the hell you figure that? You tell me—I ain't his brother. Why, Christ—look at this card? The ear on it's bent crooked-er than my dog's! And this one—this one's been folded clean in half. If that don't beat all!"

In spite of their accusatory language, the men were really only poking fun at Tom Rapp. If anything, they were thrilled that Rapp had won again because it gave them an opportunity to be loud again. As for his tampering with the cards, I had come to see it as a kind of joke among them: one player bending a card this way, the other that way: until, by now, no one knew which card was supposed to be which anymore.

"Hey, Adam!" Tom Rapp called out. The younger Rapp brother had just knocked half his winnings off the edge of the table again. And again older brother Hank was bending down to salvage what he could from the floor. "Howzabout another cup a Joe?"

Tom Rapp was looped. Obviously, he and Hank had been cutting their powder with Jim Beam on the way up. The Joe he was referring to was coffee. After I'd folded, I'd made the mistake of taking a seat beside the stove. Now, whenever one of our guests wanted another cup of Maxwell House, I had to play the part of waitress as well.

Turning to the men seated to his left, Tom Rapp added:

"Any of you girls needing a cup?"

"Oh, sure! Oh, sure!"

I refilled the cups as they came in, and then set to brewing another pot.

Swanson sat across from the Rapps, beneath the clothing net because he was the only player small enough to fit under it. His money was stacked in perfect columns of quarters, dimes and dollar bills—in sharp contrast, for instance, to the slopped heap beside Tom Rapp's right knee. Since snorting his share of the cocaine, Swanson's already natural inclination to fidget had accelerated to a remarkable degree. His fingers seemed constantly to be rearranging cards; pinching subtle creases into them; tapping the tops of them for a new draw. The cocaine had plastered a perma-grin on his face. His eyes, shifty as they were, moved from one player's hand to the next with such comic intensity that I had to control myself from laughing right out loud. Although he wasn't winning, he was holding his own.

The dealer was calling out the next hand. But to no avail. Tom Rapp was stealing the spotlight again: going on and on about the magical qualities of the perfumey hair tonic he'd greased his head with for the occasion. Apparently not one to be upstaged, the dealer, one of the men I hadn't met, smiled to himself. His pale blue eyes narrowed, glinting like metal. Then, still smiling, he reached beneath the table and, for the third time tonight, brought out his steel cowbell. I shook my head. Each time the players became too unruly, this fisherman used the device to call their attention back to the game. And each time he'd rung it, the contraption had only escalated their unruliness. All the same, the dealer, smiling ear to ear now, rang it loud and clear:

CLONG!

CLONG!
CLONG!
CLONG!
CLONG!

Not again! I thought. Call me a spoil sport . . .a stick in the mud. . .a sissy. . .what you will . . .but comical and lively as this bunch may have been. . .it was simply too much for my raw jangled sleep-deprived nerves. Enough! For everything there is a season! I was so exhausted that a perma-grin was fixed on my own face. If only I could get out from between the two Texas-sized players I was sandwiched between! I needed air. A place to think. . .

"Hey! Adam!" a voice rang out from somewhere in the hull. "Adam!"

I glanced towards the Rapp brothers, thinking it was one of them ordering another round of coffees. But the Rapps were still going on and on about Tom's hair tonic: now claiming how it drove the women wild.

"Adam!"

It was Swanson. He'd been blocked from view because the man seated next to him had stood up to run his hands through Tom Rapp's hair for good luck. I could see Swanson gesticulating behind the fisherman's backside. He was motioning me to lean closer that he might be heard.

"How you doing?"

"All right," I said. "Still tired though."

Swanson shook his head, cupping an ear.

"Tired!" I shouted—so loud that Texas on my right frowned angrily.

"I was thinking. . ." Swanson continued, leaning closer now. "Since you're just sitting there . . . how about heading out back and taking care of that small bucket of hooks you didn't get to last night. There's a good chance we'll be needing them tomorrow."

"All right," I answered, already standing up from the metal toolbox I'd been sitting on. "I'll do it."

"Hey, Phil?" I overheard a fisherman seated next to him call out. "How about loaning the big fella to me when you're done with him?"

But hadn't heard the rest of the man's lame joke or Swanson's reply as I scurried up the 5-step ladder out of the hull.

Half an hour later I sat filing hooks on the cooler out back, a Coleman lantern propped at my feet for the close work. Fog had drifted in between the time we'd dropped anchor and when I'd come out on deck, visibility at about a hundred yards. The other trawlers assembled nearby were whited-out from view.

Jacked as I was on Maxwell House and cocaine, it didn't take much to conjure up the dream of the Beast I'd had two nights running. The Beast was half-dragon and half-machine and had risen from beneath a reef to destroy the world. With gargantuan shovels at the ends of its arms and legs and a huge hydraulic winch connected to its tail (like the winches I'd seen on a giant factory trawler—only bigger), the Beast had piled through these bays and inlets and quiet coves devouring everything from the ocean floor up. While the Beast grew, the world around it diminished: until all that remained of these watery fiords and forested islands were dry steppe and tumbleweed and little muddy creeks trickling through empty canyons.

I think the Beast was a metaphor for feelings I'd been having since my talk with Sue Ann Bonnet. I was just then beginning to realize how my species had become a kind of parasite upon this earth: an invasive species destroying everything and anything that came in way of our appetites.

"Enough!" I thought aloud.

What was wrong with my species! How was it we couldn't see past our greed? Why couldn't we understand that we were fowling our own goddamn nest by not respecting this magnificent world that was our one and only home? Were our baser instincts—the weak side of my species–destined to bring doom upon us?

Hooks finished, I turned off the propane lamp. To the east, the horizon was already reddening; the stars above the distant white-capped peaks beginning to fade. In less than an hour, we'd be fishing again. Looking down at my hands, I thought how gray and plastic they looked in my lap. They no longer looked like my own: just tools now like the other men's hands. Balling them into fists, I found that it hurt to do so.

There were sounds along shore. I saw two large ravens combing the shell-strewn beach for food. The birds seemed like huge bats in the blue-gray gloom. They were in disagreement over something or other, cawing loudly. I remembered being told that seeing a raven fly in the first light of dawn was a sign of good fishing ahead.

"Just my luck!" I thought aloud.

The card party was quieting. No doubt our guests would leave soon. Then, maybe, I could con Swanson into allowing me a half-hour nap. Swanson himself was probably pretty worn out by this point.

And I was about to continue on to the wheelhouse, when I became aware of something in my periphery, something coming towards us from the water and the fog. Turning slowly in that direction, I stopped mid-turn: my mouth, no doubt, gaping wide.

"Oh, shit! Oh, shit!"

Rising out of the sea like Poseidon himself, a navy blue supply barge—at least a hundred feet high—emerged through the fog. Frozen, my eyes fixed on two large deck lights at opposite end of the barge's slanted prow, glaring down at us like the fiery eyes of the Beast I'd seen in my dreams.

Stumbling, tripping over the bucket of hooks—I finally came out of my shock. The barge was about seventy yards away, heading straight for us. There was still time to warn the others. Racing to the door of the wheelhouse, I yelled out the only thing I could think to say in brief enough terms to rouse the men:

"Fire! Fire! Everyone on deck!"

It did the trick. Punching and kicking and clawing the men below clambered for deck. I head the card-table overturn in their wake; the sound of coins flying across the room to the floor. One man cried out that he'd been bit; another that his head had been stepped on.

Rushing back outside, I climbed the ladder leading to the roof of the wheelhouse to untie our skiff. There was still time! The barge was a good sixty yards away. We might have to swim for it: but at least no one would be trapped below when the Western World went down.

The men were on deck, some even in their skiffs, hurriedly untying them from their stays. All were shouting:

"Fire? What fire?"

"No!" I shouted back, motioning towards the oncoming disaster with my head while my hands worked furiously on a knot. "No fire! The barge! It's heading straight for us!"

Swanson appeared on deck now, running right beneath me. He had an oil-smudged rag in one hand and a monkey wrench in the other. Even in the ashen light, his face was brick red, and manic. Like those before him, he was yelling "Fire?

What fire?" He mumbled something about there being no fire in the engine room.

The skiff untied, I was free to glance over my shoulder and see why the men were still standing about. The barge, which had been coming towards us at such a good clip, was stationary now, about forty yards away.

Word had been passed among the men so, in some quarters, laughter could be heard.

"Oh, shit!" Tom Rapp laughed. "Ain't no fire, Phil! It's just young Adam! He thought the barge was going to hit us!"

"Barge? Hit us? What?" said Swanson, looking from one fisherman to the next. "Don't fuck with me, you bastards! What in the hell is going on—"

"No. That's right, Phil," said another man. He pointed at the barge from his skiff, no longer paddling. "It was the kid." Grinning, he added: "Must have been smoking some pretty strong shit!"

By now I'd become aware of the long wire cable extended out of the water connected to the side of the barge. Before I could explain for myself, Hank Rapp said:

"That crazy kid of yours thought the barge was gonna wop us when it was only straying on its anchor!"

Feeling about two inches high, I descended the ladder. I wouldn't even try to defend myself. It was too stupid! A barge barreling down on an anchored boat?

Shrugging my shoulders at Swanson, I was met by a hard fist that knocked me off the last rung of the ladder to the deck.

"Get up! Get up?" Swanson said, standing over me with monkey wrench still in hand. "Get up before I smash your teeth in."

I was already crawling to my feet, grabbing hold of a rung of the wall ladder. Swanson's sharp left had come out of nowhere, like a hardball striking a sleeping infielder. Checking my mouth for blood, I found none.

"I was trying to warn you," I said.

Those fishermen still on deck had closed ranks around Swanson and me. Most were still laughing, their bead-set eyes registering FIGHT. I was careful not to appear too confrontational. First off, Swanson's punch had really done a number on my head. Second, I figured if we got in an out and out brawl, and I was somehow able to put Swanson down, the other men—with the possible exception of Tom Rapp—would side with Swanson and finish the job for him if he fell.

"Don't you ever yell fire on this boat unless you goddamn fucking mean it!" Swanson said. He'd lowered his wrench, but was still fuming.

"You tell him, Phil!" someone piped from one of the skiffs.

I cringed, forcing myself not to look in the man's direction.

"Now get your ass downstairs and clean up that hull. We're pulling anchor in half an hour."

Turning to the other men, Swanson said,

"All right. That's it, boys. Party's over. We'll split the pot between us."

Overwhelmed, but glad to have a hole to climb into, I made for the wheelhouse. By the time I reached the ladder leading down to the hull, the topic of concern among the men had become who had and who had not been winning prior to their card game's disruption.

Chapter Fifteen

A Close Call

By ten that morning I'd stopped counting. Bam! The second I'd cleared a line of one salmon and set the brake to bring in the next it was jackpot all over again. My clothes, hands, arms and face were splotched and splattered with the blood and scales of these salmon. I was literally running back and forth between the cockpit, the cooler and the holds below deck; slipping and sliding and side-stepping past disemboweled carcasses of salmon; so busy and so drunk with fatigue that the danger of what I was doing didn't occur to me. Everything was simply jerk and reflex now.

It was noon: the sun straight up, the sky a pale blue, cloudless. The seas were relatively placid: swells running across the broad green waters like a zephyr across fields of wheat. All around Esther Island came the frequent far-off flash of salmon harvested on the decks of other trawlers in the drag. Gulls chased the trawlers in tow: wheeling, swooping, and diving in our wakes for another handful of fresh-tossed innards. A gang of them flapping three feet over my head had become so aggressive that I sprang up from my crouched position over a half-gutted salmon and slashed the air with my knife and even nicked one of the birds on its leg. Cursing at the unruly birds, I stumbled back into the cockpit 15 seconds later. The trolling pole on my left was already shivering: signaling another catch.

"Damn it!" I cursed out loud.

The holds were already three quarters full. Where was I supposed to store the catch if things continued at this pace? Slamming back the release lever on the brake, I whirled in the next line.

I'd seen Swanson only twice since our 5 a.m. breakfast of peanut butter sandwiches and leftover corn chips from last night's card party. On both occasions, we'd only exchanged grunts and nods towards each other. This had been just as well with me. In spite of my old grievance that I did the bulk of the work while Swanson ogled over back issues of Hustler magazine, it was a luxury to not have to deal with his incessant nagging. My single hope was to make it through this last day on Esther Island without incident. During the three-day closure coming up, I would decide whether to quit the Western World. Even if I couldn't get anything out of Swanson for the first three weeks of work, I figured these last three days of record catches on the Island should bring me a least a few dollars. Something for my misery.

The clothespin and rubber snubber for the next tag-line were clear of the water, with reach. With the same hurriedness of movement, I re-set the brake, and then unclipped the tag from the main trolling line. Feeling the power and size of the salmon on the end of this line, I wrapped the snubber part of the tag around a forefinger and climbed out of the cockpit. I'd land this one at center deck: take no chance of losing it.

A minute later, I had the forty-pounder aboard. I was crouched over it at mid-deck, had just opened it rose-pink belly to remove the flowery innards. While scraping the excess stomach lining off one of the two flaps of meat with the side of my blade, a shadow crossed over my work. Swanson, of course. He was inspecting the catch. Leaning over the cooler, he lifted out individual salmon and began to finger the meat. Shortly after breakfast, I remembered Swanson scratching the bottom of his pipe for resins. If there was one thing I couldn't tolerate right now, it was another of his little THC fits.

"Hey! I said hey!" Swanson began—his voice with its characteristic shriek, his boots in my face. "What's going on back here? How am I supposed to sell this kind of shit? Huh? Who in the hell would buy this kind of slop?"

I ignored Swanson: flipping the forty-pounder over and scrapping stomach lining off the opposite flat of meat. Often, in the past, Swanson would simply walk away if I continued working right on through one of his little fits.

"Are you fucking blind, man?" Swanson continued—his voice making me cringe. "Look how you're butchering the meat. . ."

My hands were trembling so badly now I had to stop. All morning I had been preparing myself for just this sort of confrontation. I'd promised myself I wouldn't let him get to me. If I could just get through this last day! And here it was . . . happening all over again.

"What?" I shouted—my head still down. "Look at what?"

"The meat, damn it!" Swanson cried, furious now. He was pointing down at the pink flesh: his finger jabbing inches from my nose. "Look how you're dragging the knife all crooked along its belly. Sweet fucking Christ. . ."

I strained to see the supposed marks: but found the straining only made my eyes blur worse. From overuse or zero rest or plain dumb stubbornness, I couldn't—or refused—to see a damn thing.

"Yeah! O.K!" I shouted. "I see 'em. Big fucking deal—"

"Big fucking deal!" Swanson interrupted—his voice the same in my ear as the gull's overhead. Grabbing the forty-pounder out of my hands, he spread the flaps of meat apart and shoved it in my face. "You're fucking up my catch and all you can say—"

Swanson stopped talking with choke.

I had the collar of his flannel shirt bunched tightly in my left fist—my right fist holding the filet knife inches from his tight white turkey neck.

"Fucker!" I said, slamming him against the wall of the wheelhouse. "Fuck your fish! You hear me—fuck 'em!"

I was at once thrilled and terrified by my newfound strength. Even without the knife, I knew I could crush the life of Swanson with my bare hands. It was the old story of the master slain by the slave as the master grows soft from lack of work and the slave hard from too much.

Pushing Swanson aside, I dropped the bloodied blade: thinking, I'd come that close to killing the bastard over a fish!

Swanson leaned against the jamb of the wheelhouse door, clutching his throat, his face terribly pale.

I grabbed onto a steel cable as the Western World pitched beneath us. Out the corner of my eye I saw one of the large buoys set at various spots around Esther Island to warn boats of dangerous rocks or reefs ahead.

Swanson noticed this himself. Spitting out his plug of tobacco, he inserted a fresh one from the lid in a rear pocket of his jeans. Then, without a single word or gesture of reproach—not even a shake of his head—he returned to the wheel.

The gulls, which had flown off at the outset of our scuffle, were circling and squawking overhead again. Over my shoulder, I noticed that both trolling poles were shivering. Picking up my knife, I returned to the half-cleaned forty-pounder. I felt the trawler swing sharply aft as Swanson steered us wide of the approaching wash-rock. I wondered whether I was officially fired now or what. Apparently, not until we'd finished with today's run. I wondered whether Swanson would have me arrested. Maybe he was calling the authorities right this minute. Turning back to my work, I tried my best to not knick the meat on this salmon any more than I had already.

Chapter Sixteen

How You Ride It!

That evening, towards eight o' clock, Swanson slipped out back and announced a change of plans.

"Haul in the gear!"

He'd startled me and I tried to cover this up by sitting down on the wood siding as a large roller tipped the cockpit. All day I'd been waiting for him to try something.

"Sure," I said, setting the brake so I could face him. "What about the cooler on deck?"

The fishing had dropped off shortly after our incident at noon. The flood of salmon we'd run into earlier might have been the tail end of this three-day Fraser River run. Now that the tide was changing—and activating a feed by stirring the ocean bottom—there was a chance we could still fill the cooler with a dozen or more local Kings and Cohoes.

"Naw. . ." Swanson said, grabbing the haystack as we see-sawed over a second roller. "We'll supper tonight on a little beach I know a few miles south of here. Cook in the sand. Get out of these damn winds."

Nodding, I pushed back the hair from my eyes. A big williwaw had whipped up a few hours ago. The sun was lowering behind Swanson: putting him in a strange-silhouetted light. I thought how unlike him it was to not take every fish we could get.

"What about the catch?" I asked, turning my face away for a second as a ray of red sunlight flashed in my eyes. "Aren't we supposed to deliver it at HARRY'S tonight?"

"The catch?" Swanson repeated, as though the thought had just occurred to him. "Well. . ." He leaned into the hayrack as a third roller tipped the deck. "We'll put it off till the morning. That way we'll avoid the lines and get a fire going before dark."

From the wheelhouse came a loud squelch: someone trying to get through on the wire. Asking if this beach supper things was all right with me, Swanson took my noncommittal shrug of the shoulders as an O.K. Without another word— without any acknowledgment of the murderous scuffle that had occurred between us at noon—he returned to the wheelhouse; the hitch of his high shoulder more marked than usual because of the rolling seas.

I opted to remain out back as we approached the narrow gorge leading to the tiny bay we were to anchor in tonight. The midnight sun was still visible, hovering on the horizon, and had a wholly disorientating effect. In spite of Swanson's apparent willingness to let bygones be bygones, I detected an underlying icyness to his manner that indicated the matter was all but forgotten. It was lurking just beneath the guise of his calm surface, waiting until just the right moment to lash out for the jugular.

Having just finished packing the last of the day's catch below deck, I sat on the cooler with my fists between my legs, shivering. I wondered why, with all these easier bays and inlets to get in and out of, Swanson had chosen this one to camp at tonight. Another reason for delaying our delivery at HARRY'S was because of our vessels size we could only get in and out of this bay during high tide. High tide having occurred at 8:14, we were cutting it close as it was.

I stood as we entered the first corridor of this serpentine gorge. The sky was already a deep turquoise. Granite cliffs rose ninety feet out of the water either side of the trawler at perfect ninety-degree angles. The waters were as narrow as fifty yards across in places. And iceberg-like rocks littered the path ahead of us: jutting thirty to forty feet out of the water as we drifted by.

When we were about a quarter mile into the gorge, Swanson poked his head out the wheelhouse door and, pointing towards the gray cliffs on our right, said:

"Petroglyphs . . ."

There were about a dozen in all: strewn across the broad-faced granite walls like inner city graffiti. They were rough-hewn one-dimensional figures of men and women and whales and fish and animals. One figure stood out from the rest— about thirty yards deeper into the gorge. It was directly beneath a dwarf spruce tree growing perpendicularly out of a crevice in the cliff wall. In straight blunt lines, it depicted a man with one hand over his heart and the other over his stomach. It was the simplest and least creative of the carvings: except for the strong feelings of horror and despair it evoked out of me. There was something about the man's face that made me think he was very young and very old at the same time: a sage and a fool all at once. His eyes were wide and staring—and while his hand covered his heart—his mouth was slightly parted and drawn down in a frown not unlike that of a salmon.

Entering another corridor of this gorge . . . I began to pace deck. We were passing more of these iceberg-like rocks every two-hundred feet or so now. The limbs of the dwarf spruces growing in the crevices stretched their mangled arms out over the glossy green waters as though to reach out and touch us. Barnacles and mussels, attached to the cliffs at water level by the tens of thousands, seemed to watch us as we slid by. Forcing myself to stare directly ahead (to belay the claustrophobic feeling I had that these granite walls were actually closing in on us), I began to wonder if we'd ever make it to this fabled beach of Swanson's before wrecking the boat. I expected to feel our bulwarks come crunching in at any moment. What if Swanson had entered the wrong passage? What if this gorge suddenly ended? Or it became so narrow we couldn't proceed further? There was no way in hell we'd be able to turn the trawler around: we'd be like the proverbial ship stuck in a bottle! Finally, rounding one more dizzying bend of the gorge, the black green waters beneath us widened and we moved out onto the main body of this hidden bay.

After dropping anchor, I was told to bring the skiff from the roof of the wheelhouse. Untying the orange plastic skiff, I slid it down on my back and flip-flopped it right side up on the water with a loud smack. It suddenly occurred to me if Swanson wanted to kill me or something . . . this would be the perfect place to do it. There were probably hundreds, even thousands, of isolated little bays like this all up and down the Southeast Coast. Swanson had mentioned that only he and a few other fishermen even knew this spot existed. He wouldn't even need to do the killing with his own hands. He could simply abandon me here . . . leave me to the elements . . . the bears and wolves and lions that were said to inhabit all of these islands. If someone should come looking for me months later, what was the likelihood they would even think of searching out a place like this? Staring wide-eyed at the foliage massed in green along shore, I argued that I'd become hysterical. But why else would any normal person want to supper on a goddamn beach in a hollow like this? And why had Swanson pointed out those rock carvings to me? Surely, he was trying to spook me; toying with my stupid puny little mind.

I was still musing over these matters when Swanson emerged from the wheelhouse.

"O.K.," he said—a bag of groceries under an arm. "Get in the skiff."

I just stared at him.

This was too unfucking believable. Strict Hollywood script.

"Get in the skiff!" he repeated.

I got in.

Two hours later, I trudged up and down the shell and gravel beach searching for more firewood. It was eleven o' clock and still we had not eaten. The moon, at last quarter, had just cleared the eastern tree line: putting the hills, mountains and trees surrounding this obscure, tear-shaped bay in a dull phosphorescent light. The air hummed with quiet: the crackle of our fire, the soft lapping of the water along shore, the crunch of my own boots the only sounds reaching my ears. Fifty yards away, following me as I moved up the beach, the Western World strayed on its anchor: its white paint-chipped exterior ghost-like in the purple gloom.

Swanson had started the fire over an hour ago, but was waiting, he said, for better embers. He sat cross-legged a yard from the flames, stirring the fire occasionally with a switch he'd broken off a nearby sapling. Although he'd shown no obvious signs that he'd taken me here to do me harm, he had appeared more interested in keeping our fire well-stoked than in engaging in any of the half-dozen conversations I'd attempted to bring about.

I stopped when I came to the beached rowboat. I'd stumbled upon it earlier while taking a leak. The rowboat was half eaten away with rot, half-hidden beneath a clump of salmon-berries. Gingerly pushing aside some the shrub's thorny vines, I began to kick out pieces of wood from the skeleton of its bottom.

Along with offering a ready source of fuel, the boat had become something of a mystery to me. Its bleached weather wood had a petrified quality to it that made it hard to say just how long it had been here. It may have been only a year or two, then, just as easily, twenty or thirty years. And how had it arrived at this obscure spot? Had a fisherman seeking refuge from a downed vessel paddled here on it? The surrounding trees and mountains would have provided fortress from the rough seas and winds outside this bay. If he'd been able to forage through the summer . . . had been able fend off the bears, wolves, and lions and been able to provide makeshift shelter for himself, would he have been able to endure the long white season (seasons?) of winter? Searching distractedly though the dark bramble and underbrush outlining the beach . . . I imagined this Robinson Crusoe of mine had, indeed, survived and was running wild, half-mad on the island at this moment . . . that years of isolation from humankind had brought him to a Neanderthal state . . . that he'd learned to feed on the raw flesh of deer and fish and wild goat . . . and that he was, at this very moment, spying on Swanson and myself . . . sizing us up.

And it was while my head was full of such thoughts that the answer came to me. BURN THE WESTERN WORLD! BURN THE FUCKER DOWN! It wouldn't be hard to do. Our skiff was just yards away, both paddles still in it, almost inviting me. Swanson's back was towards me, and from where the trawler had strayed, it would be almost out of his view. I'd start it in the engine room, of course. Swanson kept gallon cans of gas there and oily rags. Splash a little Boy Scout juice around; dump out a box of matches, light a stick. By the time I was back ashore with the skiff, the first billows of smoke would be issuing from the wheelhouse—

SNAP!

A knotty piece of wood popping back at the fire, followed by cursing about the hold up on the wood. Scooping up an armload of the ivory planks, I trudged back to the fire's pit.

Swanson was removing something from the grocery bag when I arrived within the perimeter of the fire's light. I stopped in my tracks. Since the moment Swanson had appeared with the grocery bag under an arm, I'd suspected him of packing a gun inside the sack. Observing that Swanson was only moving the salmon now, I moved cautiously forward.

"Mmm. . . " I said, smiling when Swanson glanced up at me. "Salmon smells good."

Swanson nodded, but said nothing.

Dropping the wood in its designated pile, I sat across the flames from Swanson; bracing me tired back against a rock. I watched Swanson reposition the salmon, wrapped in aluminum foil, between two rocks. Then he brought out a can of beans, opened its lid with a can-opener, and placed it on a flat rock beside the salmon. He peeled off some foil from the salmon and covered the lid of the can with it. Then he resumed his cross-legged position. Once again his eyes turned towards the faint display of aurora borealis shimmering pale green, pink and blue above the northern tree line.

I shifted uneasily: kicking sand and gravel into the fire's pit. There was something too damn serene and removed about Swanson tonight. And it was not because he was stoned. He'd gone cold turkey now for over 24 hours. There was something else going on. I was sure of it. It was almost as though he was trying to lull me off guard. I was so out of it now it wouldn't take much. Already waves of sleepiness were oozing into my head in thicker and thicker waves; getting harder and harder to fight off. If I didn't try something soon—try to get to the bottom of this—it might be too late.

Clearing my throat, I asked, point blank:

"What are we doing here?"

Swanson looked down from the display of lights, his chiseled features hatchet-like in the red play of the fire.

I hesitated. Maybe it wasn't smart to make my suspicions known. Still, there was this tiredness to consider: another wave of it pressing down on me now like morphine.

"I said what are we doing here?"

I leaned forward, back straight, fully alert.

Swanson grinned horribly—his eyes narrowing into flint-like slits.

"What do you mean?"

I glanced knowingly at the grocery bag. The image of Swanson suddenly removing the revolver from the sack, and pointing the barrel at my forehead and firing from point blank range flashed through my head: causing me to kick up more sand and gravel into the fire's pit.

"I mean what's inside the bag?"

I flinched at a loud hissing noise from the fire. The butter and lemon juice Swanson had earlier placed in the salmon's belly had begun to leak through the foil. Distracted, Swanson flipped the salmon over. He opened the foil pouch, and spread the steaming butter and lemon juice more evenly with a stick. Then he closed the pouch, looking across the flames as though he had forgotten what it was we were talking about.

Again, I hesitated. What if I was wrong about there being a revolver in the bag? Surely, there were easier—legal—means Swanson could take to get his revenge. He could have simply called the Coast Guard and had me arrested on assault charges. Why risk going to prison? This whole scenario—taking me to a deserted island to off me with a .38—was no doubt a result of too many books and movies and TV. Yet . . . I couldn't help it. I had to know if there was a gun in the goddamn sack. The risk of not knowing was too great.

Suddenly, without realizing exactly what it was I was going to do, I scrambled across the sand on all fours and snatched the grocery bag right out of Swanson's hands.

"Hey!" Swanson exclaimed. "What the fuck? Give it back!"

Smiling crazily, I shuffled backwards in the heavy sand, tripping ass backwards over the pile of firewood. Scrambling to my feet, I turned the bag upside down and shook out its contents: a box of matches, some utensils, paper plates– a can of peaches.

"Peaches!" I shouted. "Where's the gun?"

"Peaches? Gun?" Swanson said, on his feet now. "What the fuck are you talking about?"

I dropped to my knees, picking up several of the items littered at my feet. I turned the bag upside down and shook it a second time. Finally, convinced there was no gun, I let the bag fall to the sand. My face burned in humiliation. I glanced towards Swanson, wishing to explain. But it was too late. Swanson had already figured it out for himself.

"Oh, shit! Oh, jeez! Oh, Christ!" Swanson exclaimed, falling to his knees doubled-up in laughter. "A gun! Peaches! In a grocery bag! Bang! Bang! Oh, man! That's the funniest fucking thing—"

But was unable to continue: overcome as he was by the situation.

Realizing how utterly ridiculous I must have appeared scrambling on all fours like a crab for the bag of groceries, I began to laugh myself. First just a little snicker; then a few more; finally whooping nearly as loud as Swanson.

When we'd both calmed down enough to talk, I wiped the tears from my eyes and stammered out the only words I could think to say:

"I guess you know I'll have to quit now."

Wiping tears from his own eyes, Swanson righted himself in the sand, and answered:

"Fine. Quit. Better yet . . . you're fired!"

I gathered up the plates and utensils I had scattered about, and after Swanson had checked the meat with a fork, we began to eat.

After a good amount of time had passed, Swanson said:

"Adam? Can I ask you a question?"

I nodded.

"All that stuff Miss Sue Ann Bonnet fed you about Mother Earth and life out of balance and thinking about future generations: You bought all that, didn't you?"

I nodded again.

There was a long pause, and then Swanson said:

"This is what I think, Adam. In the end—in the grand scheme of things– ol' Mother Earth will shake us off her like a tick off a dog's back." And, after another pause, he smiled and added:

"The trick, kid, is in how you ride the bitch."

Chapter Seventeen

Departure

I was rescued by Miss Sue Ann Bonnet and her husband, George Peterson, the next day.

After delivering our catch at HARRY'S, we headed 20 miles south to Cape Spencer. Swanson was continuing on to Sitka, but said I could catch a ride all the way back to Juneau with George and Sue Ann.

"Hello, sailor!" Sue Ann called out, waiting on deck of the Mighty Mert as our two prows played paddleball with the waves. "You and Phil giving up on the married life?"

"Hell, yes!" I said, shrugging my shoulders.

It was good to see Sue Ann again.

It was a brilliant blue September-like morning. The winds had followed us all the way down Cape Spencer: the seas white-capped, but the swells running few and far between. Sue Ann was dressed for the weather in a bright blue stocking cap and a heavy wool shirt.

When our prows got as close as they were going to get, I leaped aboard the Mighty Mert, Sue Ann grabbing me as I touched down. When she saw that I would not resist, she gave me a hug.

"Thanks, Sue Ann!" I said.

We watched as Swanson and the Western World pulled away.

"Get any dough out of the old tightwad?" Sue Ann asked—out the side of her mouth.

"A little," I said. "But not without a hassle. He wanted to send me off with two salmon!"

Sue Ann shook her head and grinned.

George Peterson came out to meet me—the Mighty Mert's engine puttering in neutral. George Peterson was a big as Old Judge Peterson, only much quieter, and gentler. He wore bottle thick reading glasses and had a Russian Orthodox-style beard. He smiled big and easy like a farmer.

"Nice to meet you, Adam," George said, shaking my hand. There was not a trace of jealousy or suspicion in his voice. I smiled back: thinking, even though George looked like the Jolly Green Giant next to Sue Ann, in a funny way, they were a perfect match. Sue Ann saw me thinking this and smiled back in appreciation.

Inside the Mighty Mert's wheelhouse, Sue Ann had fried up a batch of apple-fritters to go with our lunch of deep-fried halibut and freshly ground coffee. Looking around the inside of the Mighty Mert, I thought how refreshingly different it was than inside the Western World. It was wonderfully light and airy: George's shelf of Field Guide books on Alaska plants and animals and marine life; Sue Ann's Indian Art pieces, raven and eagle feathers, shells and beads, whale bone vertebrae, roots and dried flowers; Old Judge Peterson's handcrafted cribbage board made out of whale baleen, and a picture of Judge circa 1958 (Judge Peterson looking like a young Ted Williams, the baseball player). When I asked where Old Judge Peterson was,

George and Sue Ann simultaneously held fingers to their lips and motioned towards the hull.

"Sleeping . . ."

While Sue Ann and George discussed some private matters at the wheel . . . I slipped out back with my plate of hot fritters and halibut. Taking a seat on a milk crate against the wall of the wheelhouse, I was overcome by the beauty and interconnectedness of the world rolling round me: these watery fjords, these fantastically forested islands and these distant glacial mountain peaks all part of the great chain of life I was only then beginning to understand. And I was filled with a great sadness too, knowing even then, at just eighteen years old, I would never see a world as wondrous as this again.

I watched the Western World trail away behind us in the opposite direction. I saw Philip come out on deck—the hitch of his shoulder obvious even from this distance. He was lighting his pipe and looking in my direction. Who really knew what he was trolling for out here? The next Adam? Perhaps his greater purpose was to teach fools like me a deeper lesson about the good and evil that exists in the soul of all of us: our task to know the difference and not let the dark, the weak and the base gain the upper hand.

Who knows!

And I remembered Swanson's quip about shaking a tick off a dog's back, and knew that when she shook he'd be the last tick off that bitch's back.

Swanson: the Master of Denial, keeping constant vigil on any disturbing notions or thoughts by knocking them back with pot and booze and old-fashioned All-American stubborn-headedness. I raised an arm and waved at him. Swanson did not wave back. Throwing something overboard, he retreated to the wheelhouse; taking the wheel as the Western World came out on the first open ocean troughs, the trawler shifting side to side like an overburdened mule.

Acknowledgments

Excerpts from GONE ALASKA have appeared in the following journals (sometimes in slightly different form): Adelaide Literary Magazine, Birds Piled Loosely, Chroma, Cirque, Cowboy Jamboree, The Gambler, Gravel, KGB Bar Lit, Lampeter Review, Linden Avenue Review, The MacGuffin, Mad Swirl, No Extra Words (Podcast/Episode 85), revista Literaria CentroAmericana, Salfront, Scarlet Leaf Review, Toad Suck Review, The Vignette Review, Vine Leaves, Worker's Write!, Wilderness House and Watershed Review.

About the Author

Dave Barrett lives and writes out of Missoula, Montana. His fiction has appeared most recently in Hobart, Midwestern Gothic, Quarter After Eight and Whiskey Island. He teaches writing at Missoula College and is at work on a new novel.

www.ingramcontent.com/pod-product-compliance
Lightning Source LLC
Chambersburg PA
CBHW020021030726
47499CB00007B/2211